"I told y
So w...

That was a loaded question if Linc had ever heard one.

"I want you," he said slowly and watched as Jade's eyes grew bigger, "for one week."

"What?" she finally whispered. "Are you out of your everlasting mind?"

"I'm offering you a way out. Spend the week with me, or I'll call the police." Even to his ears the ultimatum sounded offensive. Even so, he waited with baited breath for her answer. He should've stopped, kept a reasonable distance from her but he simply couldn't. The tension crackled between them as he lowered his head until his lips were inches from her ear. "I want you for six nights in my bed and seven days at my beck and call." His tongue scraped her earlobe....

Jade melted. Heaven help her she was still attracted to this monster. And now she owed him money. She was at his mercy.

A. C. ARTHUR

was born and raised in Baltimore, Maryland, where she currently resides with her husband and three children. An active imagination and a love for reading encouraged her to begin writing in high school and she hasn't stopped since.

Determined to bring a new edge to romance, she continues to develop intriguing plots, racy characters and fresh dialogue—thus keeping the readers on their toes! Visit her Web site at www.acarthur.net.

Love Me Like No Other

A. C. Arthur

KIMANI
ROMANCE

To Damon, for your patience and encouragement.

KIMANI PRESS™

ISBN-13: 978-1-58314-793-1
ISBN-10:   1-58314-793-4

LOVE ME LIKE NO OTHER

Copyright © 2006 by A. C. Arthur

www.kimanipress.com

Printed in U.S.A.

Dear Reader,

Love Me Like No Other introduces the first of the Donovan clan to be swept away by love. The Triple-Threat Donovans are three brothers known for three things only: their breathtaking good looks, the size of their bank accounts and their inability to commit to lasting relationships.

What happens in Vegas, stays in Vegas—at least that's what Jade Vincent thinks until she's face-to-face with her college sweetheart. Now, to save her sister, she's forced to make a deal with the devil! Lincoln Donovan is tired of the life he thought he wanted, but he's too stubborn to see what that change is, until she literally falls in his lap.

I am thrilled to share Linc and Jade's story of rekindling lost love with you. Linc's story needed to be told first, not because he's the oldest Donovan brother, but because I so enjoyed watching him grow. He and Jade were meant for each other and I hope you'll agree. When you get a chance, please visit my Web site for a closer look at the Donovan clan, www.acarthur.net. And don't hesitate to share your comments about Linc and Jade via e-mail at acarthur22@yahoo.com.

A. C. Arthur

Prologue

"You need a wife."

Clenching his jaw, Lincoln tried his best to remember this was his mother he was speaking to. "I don't *need* anybody or anything."

"What good is all this success if you have nobody to share it with?" Beverly Donovan was unwavering when it came to the well-being of her children. She'd watched her oldest grow into a handsome man, an intelligent man, an entirely too serious and business-oriented man. And she didn't like it one bit.

"I have my family, unless you're planning on

disowning me because I refuse to get married." He
gave her a half smile, the one he always gave her
when he was trying to win her over. Normally it
worked. Today, however...

"Don't be fresh, Lincoln."

...her tone cut that short.

Beverly stood, brushed imaginary lint from her
pink Chanel-style suit and looked down at her
son. "Your father and I are celebrating forty years
together, son. Forty long, beautiful years of loving
and supporting each other. These have been the
best forty years of my life." She moved to him
then caressed his clean-shaven cheek. "I only
want that same happiness for you."

Beverly Donovan had a way with words. His
parents were happy. Happier than most married
folk he knew. It was only natural that she'd want
the same for her children. He loved that she cared
about his happiness and he loved that she'd never
been too busy with her own life to see to his. He
simply did not agree with her plans for his future.
"I am happy, Mom."

"That's what you think."

Chapter 1

"Craps!" the man dressed in too-tight black pants and a colorful vest with a bright red bowtie said. His expression remained dour, the way it had been for the last three hours since she'd been here.

Jade Vincent shifted. Her feet hurt. Whatever possessed her to wear slacks and pumps to a casino?

The man with the long black stick and the blank gray eyes leaned into the table, retrieving the dice—the ones that had just cost her another fifty dollars—and with a quick glance he handed them to her again.

Taking them out of his hand she looked down at the pile of chips that once represented all the free cash she had to spend—the entire three hundred and forty-two dollars.

What was she doing here?

The pale man waited for her to either roll the dice or walk away from the table.

Men, she thought with a heavy sigh. That was the simple answer to her latest dilemma. How a woman who graduated tops in her class from Harvard always managed to pick the worst men was an enigma to her. Her stomach twisted, her temples throbbing as chiming slot machines and hostesses with sing-song voices chanting "Coffee? Soda?" for the billionth time, echoed in her head. She didn't want to be here, didn't want to be in this desperate situation, but she'd never gotten what she wanted.

So with great reluctance and a silent prayer to the gods to shine favorably on her just this one time, she shook the dice in her hand then let them fall onto the green felt, watching eagerly as they tumbled and landed.

Her entire future rested on the roll of two red squares. Well, not her future. Noelle's future. Noelle Vincent, two years younger than Jade, average intelligence, a pretty face and a magnet for trouble. It was just three days ago that Noelle had come barging into Happy Hands, Jade's day spa, whining about some fiasco at the casino. Noelle, in her bubbly, never-worry-about-a-thing-because-my-big-sister-will-bail-me-out attitude, had sat in the steam bath and informed her older sister that she had ten days to come up with five thousand dollars or the owner of the Gramercy casino was going to have her thrown in jail. Jade hadn't had a moment's peace since then.

All Jade had ever wanted was to run her business and to lead a nice, quiet life.

Fate obviously had a different agenda.

Since her grandmother's death a year and a half ago Jade's life had been full of drama and stress. With Noelle usually being the cause of them both. Still, it would be unfair to blame all her recent misfortune on Noelle. A good portion could be attributed to Charles Benson. He was the man she'd thought she loved. The man she was going to marry.

Jade had planned every tiny detail of the wedding even through the grief of losing her grandmother, knowing how much the thought of her being married to a good man would have made Grammy happy. She missed Grammy terribly but would be forever thankful for the inheritance she'd left her. With that money Jade had planned to open her day spa.

Jade was going to make something of herself. Something her mother couldn't do. She was determined to be successful. Lillian Vincent died from years and years of alcohol abuse when Jade was sixteen. That's when Jade and Noelle had moved to Las Vegas, Nevada, to live with Grammy. Grammy spent many a day drilling into her head the importance of being independent and not relying on anyone but herself. In turn, Jade was spending her days drilling the same thing into Noelle's thick skull. Jade had been smart enough to get into Harvard and even smarter to know that she'd only be happy running her own business. And with Grammy's inheritance she'd planned to do just that.

Grammy used to laugh and say, "All that money I put into your college education and you come back wanting to give people massages."

But it was so much more than that. Massage therapy provided an escape, a healing for the stressors of the world, and Jade knew all about stress. Her ultimate goal was to provide a haven for people to seek when things became too difficult to bear alone.

Too bad Charles had had other plans for the inheritance. He'd suggested they get a joint account for the wedding expenses. She'd taken that one step further and added his name to all her accounts. Grammy's college education really was wasted on her because that was a colossal mistake.

Charles broke off the engagement two days before the wedding via e-mail. Two weeks after that when she was ready to get on with her life, Jade waltzed into the bank with the intention of leaving with a cashier's check for the down payment on the little building she'd found just south of the Strip, only to be told that the account had been emptied.

Jade was used to the bad luck streak that seemed to follow her around like a bad odor but felt this time she'd hit an all-time low. Luckily, the incident with Charles thickened her skin. Her full-time job as manager of a boutique supported her goal until finally nine months ago she'd opened Happy Hands Day Spa. But she hadn't turned a profit yet. Her financial advisor continued to advise that she was on the right track and that most businesses weren't completely in the black until a year or so afterwards. She was content with that assessment.

At least she was until Noelle's latest dilemma.

He was rich.
He was successful.
He was bored out of his mind.
Lincoln Donovan groaned, walked to his desk

and dropped into his chair. He needed something…a woman perhaps? For almost six months he'd slept alone. He hadn't dated, hadn't kissed, hadn't so much as brushed up against a feminine body. But that was all by choice.

Work was great. After only five years the Gramercy was now a top contender with MGM Grand and the Bellagio. Who would have thought a then twenty-five-year-old novice could pull off such a feat?

He'd known all along it would be a success. He wouldn't have had it any other way. That was his ambition speaking. It wasn't for the money because he had enough of that by birthright. The oldest son of Henry and Beverly Donovan, the next in line to inherit millions through a long line of old family money, he didn't need anything. And it wasn't for the exposure, because he could do without his name routinely appearing in the local papers. It was about being a part of something, a vision, a plan that he'd come up with. It was about having a purpose. And all his life he'd seemed to have a purpose. At least until now.

Linc wasn't one to complain. For instance, when the Gramercy opened he'd been labeled Vegas's Youngest Prince. By his second year he'd risen to the Hottest Bachelor. And just last year, with the help of his two younger brothers, he'd been dubbed the head of the Triple Threat Brothers.

Because they were rich, good-looking and single, the town had nothing better to do than stick a stupid label like that on him. Now every woman he so much as looked twice at believed she had his number and either ran quickly in the opposite direction to avoid the inevitable heartbreak or let the dollar signs rule over romantic thoughts and attempted to bleed him dry with mediocre sex and dull conversation.

No, he hadn't complained, he'd simply accepted it as fate and rolled with the punches. Now he felt as if he'd taken it long enough. There had to be something else to life, something else to work toward. The fact that he was sitting in his plush office, staring at a bunch of security monitors with a grim look on his face and an aching in his groin wasn't really making a stand in that regard.

As quickly as that thought entered his mind her face appeared on the screen. Monitor No. 7, the craps table. There was a small crowd gathered but he saw only her. A smooth, honey-toned complexion, dark hair pulled back into a tight ponytail and high cheekbones. He sat up in his chair and touched a button that allowed him to zoom in on the image.

She looked distracted, her eyes—a light shade—brown or probably hazel—moved from Reed, the dealer, back to the dice. There was no pile of chips in front of her so he assumed this was her last roll. Her fingers gripped the side of the table and her chest heaved with each breath she took. She had great breasts.

He swallowed.

Really great breasts, high and firm just the way he liked them. That ache in his groin increased and he clenched his teeth. He'd become a Peeping Tom, getting his jollies off a customer in his casino! With a moan he turned away from the screen taking deep breaths and thinking about baseball—which, incidentally, wasn't working.

He stood, crossed the floor to his private bathroom, then leaned over the sink and splashed cool water onto his face. He needed to get it together. Getting laid was easy enough, finding a woman who did more than arouse his libido seemed to be the problem. He wondered again at the sudden turn his thoughts had taken. Ever since that little confrontation with his mother he'd been thinking about what he really wanted out of life. An incessant twitching between his legs interrupted and he realized that what he really needed to do was to flip through his Palm Pilot and start dialing until he found a woman who could come and relieve him of all this tension.

A chirping sound came from his laptop and he clicked the mouse to bring the message up. With a sigh he realized it was from his mother, reminding him of his parents' fortieth wedding celebration this week. More accurately, she was reminding him that she would have a host of women lined up for him if he dared show up alone.

Everywhere he turned his thoughts were bound to return to women. Of their own accord his eyes found Monitor No. 7 again. The woman was still there, the one with the great breasts. He licked his lips just as the phone on his desk rang.

Saved by the bell.

The Pit Boss had summoned two other men. They actually looked like professional wrestlers dressed in too-small tuxedos but Jade refrained from pointing that out, most likely because at that precise moment the two oversize suits were escorting her out of the casino.

She'd crapped out…again. Her cheeks were flushed with embarrassment while her heart threatened to shatter with defeat. She'd known that gambling wasn't the answer but had promised Noelle she'd give it a try before going ahead with her original plan. The plan which had her at the mercy of a casino owner prepared to beg on her sister's behalf. For the billionth time today she swore if Noelle came to her with another problem in this lifetime she'd strangle her.

Jade loved her sister. She was the only family she had left. But she was sick and tired of bailing her out. Grammy used to say it was a shame Noelle got their father's brain—Jade was beginning to believe her—and his uncanny knack for finding trouble.

If only she still had her inheritance, she'd have money in the bank and she could have simply paid Noelle's debt. Although Grammy's voice echoed in her mind that if she never let Noelle fall how would her sister ever learn to pick herself up. Still, if she had the money... Her bottom lip trembled. But she refused to cry. She would not shed one measly tear. Charles had taken her money but she'd allowed that to happen. Her luck with men had always been horrible. Why she thought this time would be any different was beyond her. He'd done what all men do—use women then drop them. That's what her father had done the moment he found out her mother was pregnant with Noelle.

That should have been enough to warn Jade against all men, but as Grammy always said, "A hard head makes for a soft behind."

Now that hard head had her boarding an elevator on her way to meet with a stranger. To ask him for some time to come up with the five thousand dollars. According to Noelle that was a foolish thing to do but Jade figured she'd talk to him like one business owner to another. Besides, was five thousand dollars really worth filing charges and throwing a woman into jail?

The two ogres stepped off the elevator, one looking over his shoulder to make sure she followed him. She did, with her head held high. She'd asked to see the manager the moment those dice stopped rolling and she'd counted the seven dots. She planned to walk right in and ask him…for what? Three weeks? Three months? When would she have the money? He'd probably laugh in her face. Or worse, he might make her wash five thousand dollars' worth of dishes.

Maybe she'd have to wear one of those skimpy costumes and walk around offering watered-down soda and stale coffee to the guests. She could do that, but she'd catch a horrible cold from being half-naked in the very air-conditioned casino.

Beavis and Butthead, which she'd now named her escorts, stood to the side, dark oak double doors between the two of them. "What now?" she asked as she stared up at them expectantly. She wasn't a mind reader and was fairly sure that though they were huge and appeared not-too-bright, they could speak the English language.

"He's waiting for you," Beavis, the one on the right with the clean-shaven head volunteered.

Defiantly she folded her arms over her chest. "Who is?"

The men exchanged a glance then Beavis gave a crooked grin. "The Boss."

His words sounded ominous but she would not be intimidated. It hadn't escaped her that nobody bothered to tell her the man's name. It could be a woman for all she knew, not that the gender mattered. "So shall I just go in or do you want to announce me?"

Butthead, with an expression that said he was growing tired of her already, leaned over, twisted the knob and pushed the door open.

Squaring her shoulders and taking a deep breath, Jade walked into the office noticing first, the very masculine scent and second, the plush carpet that her high heels practically sank into. The door closed behind her and she turned to see if her guards had accompanied her inside. Of course they hadn't, and she was a little disappointed. As it stood now there were no witnesses. She was in the office alone with the Boss...except—her eyes scanned the lavishly decorated office—the Boss was nowhere to be found.

Shrugging she walked around the room. It was dark, but ornate. Rich mahogany molding, hunter-green papered walls, leather furniture and marble desktops boasted a masculine touch. There were two desks in an *L* shape directly in front of the huge window that from the outside was tinted gold. On the long side were a dozen monitors showing different views of the casino floor. Somebody liked to keep an eye on his money, she mused.

Crossing to the other side of the room she saw trophies and commendations presented to the casino by the State of Nevada, the Gaming Commission, the governor. Whoever the Boss was, he was pretty darn popular.

Absently sliding her hand over the smooth leather arm of the couch Jade wondered what it must be like to live in such splendor. She came from a middle-class family. They didn't starve but they didn't have a lot of luxuries, either. Now that she owned her own business that would change, hopefully. Too bad Grammy wouldn't be here to share it with her. She heard a clicking sound behind her and turned quickly…a little too quickly, because her heel caught in the deep carpet and she felt herself falling backward, arms flailing wildly.

Moments before her head would have hit the

edge of the marbled coffee table strong arms slipped around her waist pulling her back into an upright position. At the contact, slow and steady waves of heat slid through her body until warmth overtook her. He held her close, the front of her pressed securely against the hard strength of him. His masculine scent—she'd smelled it instantly upon entering the room—engulfed her, rendering her defenseless against its torture. Then she managed enough coherency to look at his face. She saw the eyes, remembered and immediately stiffened.

Linc had been admiring the view from behind. She wore black pants, tight around her hips and backside then stretching the length of what he imagined to be long, gorgeous legs. Her hair swayed seductively down her back as she moved. Then she'd reached out, touched the couch and let her fingers glide along the fabric. He imagined that hand moving over him in the same manner. Touching him lightly, gripping him… He took a deep breath then steadied himself before speaking.

She owed him money. This was no longer about his immediate attraction to her, but more about business. And Linc never let anything get in the way of business.

Then she'd tripped and he'd rushed over to keep her from falling. Without thinking twice he'd grabbed her, wrapped his arms around her and pulled her close, keeping her there. Those luscious breasts rubbed against his lower chest and he wanted to moan. One hand was dangerously close to the small of her back, where the roundness of her bottom began. Every inch of his body stood at attention including the one he'd been battling with since the moment he'd first glimpsed her over the monitor. He was sure she was aware of his aroused state and wondered what thoughts were going through her mind.

He looked down into her face. Noted the high cheekbones, the hazel eyes, the succulent lips...then back to the eyes again...

"Jade?"

She opened her mouth to speak but nothing came out. It couldn't be. Please, please, please, don't let her luck be *that* bad.

It had been years. Eight years to be exact. She'd thought of him occasionally—okay, frequently—in that time. But she never, ever thought she'd see him again. She didn't *want* to see him again.

But here he was, as tall, dark and breathtakingly handsome as he'd been that night. He'd developed. Instinctively her fingers tightened over his biceps. She gasped and pulled her hands away as if she'd been burned. He still held her close. Too close. She wriggled trying to break free.

"Sweetheart, that's not such a good idea right now," he said through clenched teeth.

She halted as the knowledge of what he meant poked her stomach. He had grown. She swallowed then summoned the courage she seemed to have left at the door and tried again to speak. "Then why don't you be kind enough to let me go?"

"I'm not real sure I want to do that."

His smoldering gaze held her still, reducing her insides to mush that shifted and swirled in a fiery ball at her center. Her knees were shaking. She hated herself for this pure feminine weakness. He no longer had this type of control over her, no man did. Planting her palms firmly on his chest and trying like hell to ignore the blessed rigidness beneath her palms she pushed against him. "I don't care what you want."

He frowned, then loosened his grip until his hands were no longer on her. But not before letting them glide down her hips, just brushing past her bottom. Her body quaked one last time as she took a shaky step backward.

"Fine. We'll get right to business then." He spoke as he turned away and moved around his desk.

She watched him walk—correction, Lincoln Donovan had never walked, he swaggered. That self-assured glide that said he was the man and you'd better not dispute it. His dress pants were expertly tailored and hung over his hips and taut buttocks just right. Her mouth watered. He wore all black. His pants, his shirt, his tie, everything was black and domineering. And Jade had never loved the color more. His arms were even thicker when she looked at them from a distance, his chest broader, his shoulders squared. He was built like a quarterback, his skin the color of aged rum, dark and satisfying. Damn, he was still fine.

And he was still the man who'd taken her virginity then left her high and dry the next morning.

"Business? What are you doing here?" she asked when she'd found her voice again and stopped ogling him like some schoolgirl with a crush.

"I should ask you the same thing." He took his seat then with a nod motioned for her to do the same.

She didn't want to sit. She wanted to get away from him as quickly as possible. But that would prove she was afraid. And she'd be damned if she gave him that satisfaction. She sat in the chair across from his desk. "Casinos are open to the public."

He sat back in the chair eyeing her carefully. "That they are. But they don't give away money. At least *my* casino doesn't. And according to my Pit Boss you want to speak to me about a five-thousand-dollar marker owed. How do you plan to pay? Cash or credit?"

Oh, God, this was *his* casino. Lincoln Donovan owned the Gramercy. She truly did have bad luck! Still, she refused to break down. There was a solution, she just had to find it. "I don't have that much cash on hand. I can sign a promissory note and…"

He was already shaking his head negatively. "I don't take promissory notes."

She cocked her head to the side. "But you don't have a problem taking innocent girls?" She hadn't meant to say that. Yes, as a matter of fact she had. She hadn't ever planned on seeing him again, so all the anger she'd had that morning when she'd awakened to an empty bed in a male dormitory came rushing back with a vengeance. Over the years she'd thought of a million ways she wanted to curse him out for what he'd done to her.

He frowned. "I'd rather we talked about business."

"That's fine. But our first order of business is the past. You know, the night you seduced me and the morning you left?"

"Jade—" he began.

"How could you be so careless? So evil?"

He stood, slamming his hand down on the desk. "That's enough!" he roared. "I am not going to rehash the past with you. It happened. Get over it."

"Get over it?" She stood, too, glaring at him with a look so vicious that it probably matched his. "Who the hell do you think you are? You can't just do what you want and think you don't have to ever answer for it."

He came around the desk towering over her until she had to crane her neck to keep eye contact. "I *can* do what I want. And I don't have to answer to you. On the other hand, if you don't come up with my five thousand dollars I can call the LVPD and they can engage you in a question-and-answer session."

At that moment she hated him more than she'd ever hated another human in her life. She wanted to slap him, to scream at his callousness, his arrogance. But she'd been raised better than that. So with a deep breath and a step back she decided to forego the fact that Lincoln Donovan would forever be on her most-hated list and handle her business. "I told you I don't have the cash. So what do you want?"

That was a loaded question if Linc had ever heard one.

She was beautiful. Too beautiful for words.

But then he'd known that years ago. What he
didn't know, or perhaps hadn't had the chance to
experience, was how sinfully sexy she became
when she was fired up. He'd wanted nothing
more than to grab her, to toss her over his desk
and have his way with her. Luckily, like Jade, he
remembered their past. In the instant he'd
touched her the memories of their one night
together came barreling back. He'd noticed her
weeks before they'd actually met and had
watched her the entire time she was at the party.
He'd known then that he wanted her in his bed.
It wasn't until after he'd achieved that feat that the
trouble began.

Jade Vincent was incredible to look at. Who
would have guessed that he'd want more? He had
no idea that spending one evening with her would
incite feelings of permanency that would scare
him witless.

But that was then.

And this was now. Did she have any idea how
much her words had turned him on? No, she was
clearly too angry to see that.

This was a totally different Jade than he remembered. She didn't have that naive look about
her anymore. Her body had filled out more, her
stance had become more self-assured and assertive.

No, this was definitely not the college girl he'd slept with.

And yet, he desired her just the same.

"I want you," he said slowly and watched as her eyes grew bigger. "For an entire week. Seven days and six nights." The thought came to him as simply as his next breath.

"What?" she whispered.

"I'll clear your debt if you spend the week with me."

She was already shaking her head negatively backing further away from him. It wasn't her debt, but he didn't need to know that. He didn't need to know anything about her. "You are out of your everlasting mind."

She moved and he moved with her until her back was to the wall, her front dangerously close to his. "I'm making you an offer. Spend the week with me or I'll call the police." To his own ears the ultimatum sounded stupid and offensive and he waited with baited breath for her to answer.

He should have stopped, should have kept a reasonable distance from her but simply couldn't. The tips of her breasts brushed against his chest and tension fairly crackled between them. "Six nights, in my bed." He lowered his head until his lips were scant inches from her ear. "Seven days at my beck and call." His tongue scraped her earlobe.

* * *

Jade melted. Heaven help her she was still attracted to this monster. And now she owed him money. Simply put, she was at his mercy.

Even so what he was suggesting was ridiculous. She wasn't for sale…her body wasn't for sale. "No," she stated in a shaky voice.

He traced a scorching path down her neck with his tongue. "And you don't strike me as a woman who would renege on her debts."

Chapter 2

"Seven days and six nights," Jade stated matter-of-factly.

Linc was still kissing her neck but the shift in her tone stopped him. A moment ago she'd been breathless, feeling the same attraction that he was, the same attraction that they'd shared eight years ago. He couldn't believe he could still want her with the same urgency as a young, horny student. He had to get a grip on his actions, on what he was about to do, but couldn't help being entranced by the woman in his arms.

He pulled back until he could once again look

into her eyes. She had deep, compassionate eyes. Eyes that held secrets and sadness. He'd always wanted to know why. Jade Vincent had intrigued him from the moment he first saw her. Linc was shocked to realize that eight years later her effect on him hadn't changed.

"My parents are celebrating their fortieth wedding anniversary this week. There are a lot of activities planned and I'll need a date. For reasons I won't go into I need a woman to give the appearance of a healthy, loving relationship."

"I find it very hard to believe that you can't find a date," she quipped.

Reaching out a hand he let his thumb trace her bottom lip, the very spot he longed to taste. Linc forced himself to be cautious, to take this twist of fate slowly. Eight years ago he'd let her slip away and for the last ten minutes he'd been thinking of any reason he could to keep her here.

"I can get a date. But this calls for something a little less dramatic. You'll be doing a job, working off your debt."

Jade folded her arms over her chest, effectively ending the intimate contact between her breasts and him. She looked up, defiance clear in those sultry eyes. He was curious as to what was going on in that pretty little head of hers but decided to wait until she divulged her thoughts, which, if he remembered her correctly, he was sure she'd do. Jade didn't mince words. That was part of the reason he'd left his dorm room while she was sleeping.

"A business deal of sorts?"

Her understanding didn't surprise him. Jade was a very intelligent woman. "Exactly." He nodded.

She tilted her head, placed a finger to her chin and gazed at him steadily. "I'll stay with you for seven days and six nights. I'll smile and act like I have some semblance of admiration for you." She paused then slipped from between him nd the wall. "But I will not sleep with you. For that you'll have to hire a professional. And if you call the police I'll tell them you propositioned me for money."

Linc had turned to face her and couldn't help but gape while she spoke. The more he looked at her, the more alluring she became. She'd been pretty enough to catch his attention from across the room at the frat party. That's how she'd ended up in his bed. And now, he could hardly focus on his so-called business deal as thoughts of having her back in his bed nagged at him. The strange thing was, in the very back of his mind, if he allowed himself to admit it, there was something else bothering him about Jade and her appearance at his casino.

She'd countered his offer with one of her own. He had to smile. That was precisely what he would have done. "Did I proposition you before?" he asked out of curiosity.

"You said that was the past. We're not here to talk about the past. Remember?" Jade stood perfectly still mentally willing her legs not to shake and her voice not to crack. She had to get away from him or else all her thoughts would have turned to mush, as his tongue moving sinuously over her sensitive skin had raised the room temperature several degrees already. "This is a job and those are my terms."

She'd deal with her traitorous body later. Right now she needed to deal with Mr. You're-in-debt-to-me-so-you'll-do-whatever-I-say. He might run a big, fancy casino and he might be filthy rich and he might even be too handsome for his own good, but he would *not* control her or her emotions ever again.

He smiled. Not a happy smile that reached his eyes, but a half smile that gave a slight peek of straight, white teeth. He slipped a hand into his pocket, pulling her gaze instinctively to his midsection. He was still hard, all of him. She licked her lips at the memory of his rigid erection between her thighs.

She took another protective step back although

he hadn't made any motion toward her. "So," she began a little shakier than she wanted to sound. "Do we have a deal?"

If it were possible Linc would swear her counter-offer had increased his desire for her. The simmering heat at his groin wanted him to accept the deal on the table even though it didn't include that certain satisfaction he was aiming for. She'd backed up to his desk now and was leaning against it, her hands gripping the edge, her breasts heaving, beckoning him.

Without another thought he moved closer until his erection pressed against her belly again. She leaned back, possibly to escape the inevitable. Still he leaned closer until his lips hovered above hers. His tongue stroked her top lip. She moaned. He traced the bottom lip. Her nails scraped the top of the desk. Then he covered her mouth, pressing his tongue against her lips until another moan tried to escape granting him access. Delving into the warmth Linc allowed himself a taste of the days ahead.

Memories came flooding back as his tongue, thick and hot, grazed hers, pulling her deeper until she had no choice but to cooperate. Jade felt as if she were drowning and he was her only lifeline. He controlled the kiss, controlled her, his mouth moving seductively over hers evoking a fresh wave of heat that centered between her legs.

He was thick and hard against her and she wanted nothing more than to spread her legs and let him in. The ache in her center increased as he pushed against her. He wanted her to feel him, to want him. He knew what her reaction to him was, just as he'd known all those years ago.

He'd kissed her before. Her senses froze, her heart pausing as she recalled the differences between now and then.

His tongue probed deeper, stroked more boldly over hers. Dizziness enveloped her as she clung to the wondrous feel of his hot tongue mingling with hers. Desire swept through her like a raging storm leaving her weak and submissive—two emotions she absolutely despised.

Then as quickly as the kiss had begun it ended. He pulled away. "It's a deal."

Leaving her, Linc moved around his desk. He pulled out the top drawer then retrieved a card. He reached into his back pocket and extracted his wallet. He handed her two cards. "This is the key to my penthouse here at the casino and this is a credit card."

When she'd regained her senses from that kiss she looked down at what he was giving her. "What's the credit card for?"

"There will be a formal party on Saturday, luncheons throughout the week and various other activities. You'll need a wardrobe."

A bit insulted by his words she frowned. "I have clothes."

"I'm sure you do. Think of this as your uniform for the job."

Oh, he was a smug something, an arrogant and self-assured brut that she would cut down the very next time he thought to touch her. She'd do this job because her sister's freedom depended on it. But that was all this week was about.

With a sly smile she took the cards from him. "I love a shopping spree."

"Then by all means enjoy yourself. I have meetings the rest of the afternoon. We'll have dinner in the room and we'll leave for my parents' estate in the morning."

"Where do they live?" Eight years ago she'd known nothing about him except his name and that he was the most beautiful man she'd ever seen. She wasn't surprised that a part of her still wanted to know more about him.

"Northeast of the city limits. It's a horse ranch, one of my father's new hobbies. Do you ride?"

She looked at him, and noted the hint of desire still shadowed in his eyes. He wanted her and to a certain extent he'd gotten her. She'd be at his side for an entire week. She'd made it clear that she wouldn't sleep with him, but she wouldn't pass up an opportunity to make him suffer the same way she had. "Wouldn't you like to know," she said with a half smile before sashaying out of his office.

The moment the door closed Linc let out a long, slow moan. He'd never been this hard, this excited over a woman before. When he'd kissed her he'd thought of nothing else but ripping her clothes off, getting his mouth on those breasts, those nipples that he'd felt harden beneath him. Did she ride? She had ridden him that night with the experience of a shy virgin. He'd coaxed her until she'd found her rhythm, until she'd driven him so wild he'd had no choice but to end the sweet torture.

She would ride him again, he thought, his hand resting on his erection. She would definitely ride again.

But that was for later. For now he had to handle some details. He had never taken a woman home to his parents and his brothers would surely get a kick out of the first time. Lifting the receiver he dialed his youngest brother's number.

"Speak to me," Adam answered in his deep, cheerful voice.

"It's Linc. We need a conference."

"What's up?"

"It's about this week."

"Cool. Hold on. I'll connect Trent."

After a few clicks all three of the Donovan brothers were on the line. The Triple Threat as they'd been dubbed. Each one of them, Lincoln, Trenton and Adam, separated by two years each, possessed bone-deep good looks, quick minds, huge bank accounts and the ability to make any woman whimper with need. They were also confirmed bachelors. A fact that had long since plagued the women of Nevada.

"What's going on?" Trent asked first.

Adam answered, "I don't know, big brother initiated the conference."

"I wanted to give you guys a heads up. I'm bringing someone with me this week."

"Home? You're bringing a guest home with you?" Adam asked.

"Yes."

"I assume this guest is a woman," Trent offered.

"Yes. It's a woman. Her name is Jade Vincent. She'll be spending the week with us."

"And who is this Jade Vincent?" Trent was an ex-Navy Seal who now owned a company of special investigators that filled high priority government assignments. He trusted no one and suspected everybody.

"An old college friend I ran into today."

"You haven't seen her since college and you're bringing her home to meet the folks? That doesn't sound like you," Adam surmised.

"It's not like that. It's business," Linc replied.

On the other line Trent frowned. "Explain."

"She owes me a favor and I'm collecting by using her as a shield between Mom and all the eligible ladies she'll have lined up for me."

Adam chuckled. "Good thinking."

"Whew, I sure am glad you're the oldest."

Linc frowned at Trent's words. "And why is that?"

"Because you're the first one she wants to marry off. Which leaves Adam and I more time to prowl the herd."

"I am *not* getting married. This is just a buffer for the week. Next week I'll be prowling right beside the two of you."

So she'd accepted this ridiculous arrangement to keep her sister out of jail. Noelle better be damn grateful to have a sister like her. It had taken years for her to to get over what Lincoln Donovan did to her and now in the span of a half hour she'd been reduced to that brokenhearted college girl all over again.

Except now she was not only older, she was

wiser. She would not be succumbing to his charms or his smile or his scent. She was stronger than that. She'd do this so-called job and she'd walk away from him the same way he'd walked away from her.

With credit card in hand she sat back against soft leather seats as Mario, Linc's personal chauffeur, drove down the the Strip. After Mario had indicated he'd been instructed to take her anywhere she wanted to go, she quickly directed him to the Fashion Show Mall where she did her best window shopping. There were things in the window at Neiman Marcus that she'd had her eye on for a while now.

Lately, all her money went back into the spa or toward Noelle's college education. Noelle was definitely going to set a record for how long she would draw out a four-year degree program. Jade was no fool—she was sure Noelle was stalling. While she sympathized with Noelle's fear of responsibility she wasn't footing the bill beyond this year. Now she felt like a child at Christmas who'd been given the key to Santa's workshop. Sure, this key came with lots of strings, but she wasn't going to think about that right now. The car came to a stop and she smiled to herself. Oh, no, she was thoroughly going to enjoy this moment and she'd deal with the rest later.

Three hours later her feet had begun to feel numb, the muscles in her arms strained from the weight of the bags she carried from one store to the next. She was making her way back to the car for her fifth drop off when she figured she'd better call Noelle before she sent the cavalry out to find her.

"Hello?" Noelle answered her cell on the first ring.

"Hey, it's me."

"Where are you? I thought you'd be back hours ago. Did you get the money?"

Jade rolled her eyes. She should at least be proud that Noelle had asked about her before the money. "I'm at the mall."

"That means you got the money!" Noelle said excitedly. "That's cool. What mall? I'll meet you there."

Noelle liked to shop, too. That's another reason she couldn't concentrate on school—because she was too busy keeping up with the latest fashions.

"No. Don't bother. I'm just about done. Look, I'm going away for the week. I need you to take over at the spa." Jade had been grooming Noelle for an assistant manager position and although Noelle was mostly resistant to the idea she'd caught on fast and Jade trusted she could handle the responsibility for a week. Besides, Kent, her full-time assistant, would be there should any problems arise.

"Where are you going and how come you get to go shopping and I don't?" Noelle whined.

"Because I'm the one who sold my soul to the devil to save your ungrateful behind."

"What are you talking about?"

Jade sighed. She really didn't want to give Noelle too many details. "Nothing. Just take care of the shop for the week and when I come home be prepared to have a plan for your life because I don't intend to do this for you anymore."

"Do what?" Noelle screeched. "What are you doing that you have to be secretive about? Did you rob a bank or something?"

"Girl, stop playing. I met with the casino owner like I told you I would and now I have to work for him for a week to clear your debt."

"Uh-uh, Jade, you are not stripping in some casino."

Jade almost laughed at that ludicrous statement. "No. I'm not stripping. I'm going to attend some parties with him."

"Like a call girl?"

"No! Not like a call girl. I'm not having sex with him!" No matter how much his body begs me to. "Parties, dinners, stuff like that for the week and that's all."

"Who came up with that idea? I know it wasn't you. And is he at least good-looking? I'd hate for you to be stuck with a dog for the week on my account."

"He's not ugly, Noelle." Quite the contrary. "Anyway the deal's been made."

"Jay, I don't know. I don't like how this sounds. I can go to the bank and apply for a loan," she offered.

"Noelle, you work ten hours a week at the spa. You don't make nearly enough to pay back five thousand dollars plus interest. At that rate it would take you a lifetime. It'll be fine. It's only seven days." Seven days with the sexiest man in the state of Nevada.

"I'm sorry for getting you into this, Jay."

Jade softened thinking about her baby sister instead of that man. "I know you are, Noelle. Maybe next time you'll think more carefully before you do things. I'm not going to be there to bail you out the next time."

Jade felt bad that Noelle was now crying but didn't speak. Noelle had gotten away with those crocodile tears for way too long.

"I'll work at the spa all day, every day until you get back," Noelle offered.

"Thank you. I'll call you later tonight when I settle in."

"Okay. And Jade, what's this guy's name? You know, just in case."

Jade knew she didn't have to consider a just in case. Linc was not *that* type of man. But she hated telling Noelle this. "It's Lincoln Donovan. I gotta go. I'll call you back." She disconnected before Noelle could respond.

If anybody else knew the pain and heartache Linc had put her through Noelle did. And thinking of that pain and heartache Jade did something she didn't often do, but had done once already today. She thought of revenge.

"Where to next, Ms. Jade?"

Mario was a huge man. Linc must have employed every ex-wrestler in the Las Vegas area. But after chatting with Mario amiably on their way to the mall Jade found he was quite likable. He was older, maybe nearing his fifties; only the sprinkle of gray at his temples gave that away. He wore gold rings on both his pinkies and a diamond stud in his left ear. He, Jade decided, was like somebody's father dressed like a gangster, and she liked him instantly.

With her plan for revenge foremost in her mind she said, "I need some pampering, Mario. I want to visit the best, most lavish spa in Vegas." Of course, whatever the spa she went to it would only be the next best thing to Happy Hands, she thought.

"That would be at the Bellagio," Mario said quickly. "But don't tell the boss I said that." He chuckled.

Jade smiled, too. She really did like Mario. "It will be our little secret." He was leading the way to the back door of the limo when she stopped and reached into her new Gucci bag, also courtesy of Linc's VISA.

"I almost forgot. I bought you something."

Mario held the door open and turned to face her. "Me? You're supposed to be shopping for yourself."

She waved his words away. "I know but there's only so much I can buy myself. Besides, I saw these in Saks and knew they'd look great on you." Standing on tiptoe she slipped the dark sunglasses onto his face, pushing them up his nose with a slender finger, then stood back to survey him. "Perfect!"

Grabbing the lapels of his black jacket Mario posed one way, then turned another. "I feel like Dan Aykroyd in *The Blues Brothers*."

Jade laughed. "You look ten times better."

With a lavish swing of his arm Mario motioned for her to climb in. She did and sat back against the seat again, this time thinking of the massage she was going to get. She'd been to the Spa at Bellagio once before, a special treat to herself. In addition to the extravagant decor and the pleasant staff, she'd fallen in love with the Ashiatsu Oriental Bar Therapy. As if they could read her mind, her toes, which had been crumpled inside her pumps for the last seven hours, screamed for mercy!

Ashiatsu ("ashi" meaning foot and "atsu" meaning pressure) was an ancient form of body work using deep compression. A "push, pull, pumping" effect worked the muscles of the spine. Jade swore by its healing tendencies. She'd learned the technique at the Nevada School of Massage Therapy where she'd obtained certification as a massage therapist. Grammy thought rubbing on strange bodies was crazy but Jade loved it. Ashiatsu was a specialty at Happy Hands and her clients loved it.

Within a half hour she'd removed all her clothes and had donned the thick, soft Bellagio robe. She'd had a mini foot massage and was now lying on a massage table with a thin, stern-faced therapist above her, holding on to bars attached to the ceiling. The moment his feet came down on her back she was in heaven.

Another hour and a facial later and Jade was as relaxed as they come. She remembered what was next on her agenda. Dinner and then a night at Lincoln's place. While she wasn't particularly afraid of the dinner she didn't want to rush spending the night with him. For seven days she'd be in his presence. She at least wanted tonight to herself. Her brow furrowed as she looked through the tinted windows deciding what she would do.

With a spurt of defiance she instructed Mario to take her back to her apartment. Lincoln Donovan could eat dinner alone tonight.

Linc was fuming. He'd arrived in his room expecting to see her, craving the sight of her. He'd thought of her all afternoon. Bewitching eyes, supple lips and those breasts... He'd been distracted in each of his meetings. But it wasn't just Jade physically. There was something else. He'd noticed it earlier when he'd seen her and he'd thought about it continuously throughout the day. She was different and yet a part of her seemed the same. He found himself wondering what she'd been doing over the years and who she'd been doing it with. He hadn't taken the time to get to know her when they were in college. Back then the power she had over him was too much for him to deal with. He didn't want any distractions from his business goals. But now, he wanted to take his time getting to know her, sampling her, experiencing her. Too bad he only had one week.

One of the things that was particularly worrisome was the fact that she was indebted to the casino for five thousand dollars. He'd watched her betting over the monitor. She was what they called a conservative gambler. She placed one chip on the line at a time. One fifty-dollar chip if he remembered correctly. She would have had to have spent an entire day at the craps table to get anywhere near five thousand dollars. Besides, Jade seemed too smart to loose that type of money in a casino. But that was simple enough to discover. A call to his Pit Boss would give him that answer.

His day had progressed painfully slowly, most likely because he wanted it to go fast. He took care of mundane tasks then called his manager to give last-minute instructions for his week away. One entire week was the longest he'd ever been away from the Gramercy. It was going to be difficult but he was sure that being with Jade would pass the time quickly.

Linc remembered the feel of her, soft and accommodating; and the taste of her, sweeter than any dessert his casino offered. He remembered her smile and the way her eyes, her nose, had crinkled when she'd taken her first swig of beer. That night at the frat party she'd bewitched him. He'd wanted her fiercely and had gotten her.

Tonight, he still wanted her.

So he'd moved quickly to get to his penthouse, to get to her. Only to find that she wasn't there.

Okay, so maybe she was late. He decided to take his shower and change. An hour later when he was still in his penthouse alone he knew she wasn't coming. A call downstairs informed him that Mario had returned to the hotel, without his guest, over two hours ago. In minutes Linc was stepping off the elevator heading out of the casino. Mario stood from his perch against the limo as he approached.

"Where is she?"

Mario shrugged. "Told me to take her home."

Linc gritted his teeth then yanked the handle to the back door not waiting for Mario's assistance. Mario followed his boss's lead and climbed into the driver's seat. With a glance in the rearview mirror he asked where to.

Linc answered with a scowl. "Take me to her."

Mario did as he was told, weaving through the early evening traffic in the direction from which he'd just come.

She was a stubborn one, Linc mused from his seat in the back of the vehicle. When they'd first met she'd seemed amiable enough, but then they'd both had a few drinks by that point. He remembered clearly the assessing way she'd looked at him when he proposed a private party in his room.

He'd felt that same desperation, that same paralyzing need for her to say yes then, just as he had earlier today.

What was it about her?

And why on earth was he chasing her?

Even with his reputation he had an endless choice of women. But none of them had ever stirred him like Jade did.

He didn't have time to search for an answer as the car had stopped in front of an apartment building he assumed was where she resided. Linc stepped out after Mario had opened his door. Surveying his surroundings he noted that this wasn't one of the best neighborhoods in the city. It wasn't the worst but for some reason he had a hard time picturing Jade here.

"I took her bags up to 3C," Mario volunteered in a stiff voice.

Linc nodded then took the few steps leading to a rusted wrought-iron gate serving as the entrance.

The elevator was taking too long and Linc's patience was wearing thin, so instead of losing his temper—which he often did—he found the door to the stairs and headed upward.

Jade had just emerged from a soothing chamomile bath topping off her state of pure relaxation. Wrapped in her kimono-style robe she padded barefoot across the wooden floors to the kitchen. Through the open window she heard the rumblings of nightlife awakening on the outskirts of the Strip.

Women of the night and their employers would hit the streets as soon as the sky darkened completely while from a distance the glitz and glamour of the Strip would beckon all with at least a nickel in their pockets. An enticing trap, she thought to herself.

As was Lincoln Donovan.

She'd accepted his deal for one reason and one reason only—to save her sister.

This was the last time, she'd told herself, and now had told Noelle. She'd help her sister out of this jam and then Noelle would be on her own. She refused to spend her time making money just to spend it all on Noelle and her crazy lifestyle. Why her sister thought she could go and gamble with money she didn't have was beyond Jade's imagination. Still, she felt compelled to help her. They were all each other had in the world. That had been her excuse all these years even though Jade was sure that if Grammy were here she'd be telling her to let Noelle sink or swim on her own. The next time that's exactly what she panned to do.

But for now she'd made a deal.

With Lincoln Donovan.

Eight years ago she'd been young and in lust. Now she was older, wiser. This was a business deal and nothing else. Hence the reason she'd killed those dinner plans. Linc needed a date for his parents' festivities. Well, those festivities hadn't begun yet. Therefore, there was no need for them to spend time together.

That coupled with the fact that she detested being pushed around. When a man wanted to have dinner with a woman, the normal route was to ask. He'd told her and she'd showed him differently. She smiled smugly and wrenched open the freezer.

"So who was the winner again?" she asked as she frowned at three neat stacks of frozen meals. She had a large variety since this was what her complete diet consisted of, but tonight, for some reason, chicken and broccoli fettuccine just didn't sound appetizing.

A hard knock at the door had her nearly jumping out of her skin. And when she'd made her way across the room to pull it open that same skin began to heat instantly.

Her throat went dry as her gaze rested on Linc's wide shoulders completely filling the tiny doorway. He looked ominous, foreboding and commanding dressed in all brown, glowering at her as if she'd just stolen something from him.

Jade squared her shoulders and took a deep breath. "Can I help you?"

His gaze raked over her in a way that left her feeling naked and exposed and she instinctively regretted the question.

Linc cleared his throat. "We had dinner plans," he said gruffly.

"No, you had dinner plans. I went shopping and came home."

"I thought it was understood that we were staying at the hotel."

"You're staying at the hotel. I have a home, thank you very much," she quipped.

He gave an exasperated sigh. "Can I come in?"

"No," she said quickly.

"Jade?"

It was her turn to sigh just before stepping aside and allowing him entrance. "What are you doing here?" she asked, closing the door behind her.

"As I said, we had dinner plans."

She was instantly uncomfortable as she watched him peruse her apartment. It wasn't a hovel by any means but Jade was positive it was below Lincoln Donovan's standards. Just as she'd always been.

"And you left this in the car."

His voice interrupted the beginnings of her pity party and she looked down at his outstretched hand.

"Oh," she said then reached for the necklace. "It must have fallen off."

Before she could take it from him Linc pulled his hand back. "Was it a gift from someone special?"

She blinked wondering why he'd asked. "From Grammy. I mean, my grandmother."

He nodded, profoundly relieved that it wasn't from a man. He looked down at the necklace in his hand then back at her. "The clasp is broken."

Jade reached for the necklace again. Since his arrival it had become increasingly harder for her to breathe. She feared his large form simply took up too much space in her small apartment. She had to get him out of here as quickly as possible. "I'll have it fixed."

"I'll take care of it," he said simply then slipped the necklace into his pocket. "I'm hungry. Can we go to dinner now?"

Jade opened her mouth to speak then quickly closed it again. He'd asked her nicely this time, his voice velvety smooth as his gaze bore through her. She didn't know how to respond.

"Are you hungry, Jade?"

"Ah…I…I'm not dressed for dinner," she croaked. Damn, he was getting to her again. She looked down at her robe that had begun to gape a bit at her chest. Hastily she pulled it closed then cinched the belt around her waist.

Linc followed her gaze. "I'm certainly not complaining about your attire but you might want to change just in case other people get the wrong idea."

"I most certainly am not going out like this. I'm not going out at all. Our deal doesn't start until tomorrow."

"I think you're mistaken." Linc took a step closer to her. "Our deal started the moment you took my credit cards and hit the mall."

Jade thought about what he'd just said, recognized the logic and could have kicked herself. Again she reminded herself why she was allowing him back into her life. It's only for a week, she told herself—seven days and six nights then she'd have what she wanted and he could go back to his rich, polished life. The one she'd never be a part of.

"Fine," she snapped. "I'll change."

He nodded his approval as she stalked past him.

She'd change all right and Lincoln Donovan would regret coming here forcing her to do this tonight. While she wasn't financially or socially in his league, she had one positive thing going for her—she was a woman.

And he was definitely a man.

A man that wasn't above being tortured.

* * *

She wore red, come-and-get-me red, that fit her like a second skin. He swallowed as he reached for her hand to help her out of the car. The drive back to the Gramercy had been one of hell on earth. Her scent was intoxicating, coupled with that barely there dress. His blood pressure had steadily begun to rise.

They'd talked amicably in the car, she seemingly without a care in the world while he struggled to keep from blabbering how much he wanted her. They walked through the lobby, Linc noting the stares both from his staff and the guests milling about. He didn't like that. He'd never really cared before that people watched him, made conclusions about him that were false and unfounded. But the thought of them wondering what was going on between him and Jade didn't sit well with him at all.

She wore light makeup. A gold frost on the lips, something to darken her eyes and that was it. Her hair had been pulled up to a pile of luminous curls. She looked absolutely delicious and he was ravenous.

"I thought we were having dinner in the room," she said with a pretty smile.

"We'd better stay in public for as long as possible," Linc said through clenched teeth.

He escorted her to the restaurant and then to a booth reserved especially for him in the back. Sitting down, she picked up the menu. "I hear the food here is fabulous."

For endless moments Linc couldn't speak. He'd watched the sway of her hips as she walked. Then she sat while he remained standing. Her dress was cut low, very low. The view of those luscious mounds had all the blood rushing from his head. He gripped the back of the chair to steady himself then lowered his quaking body down into the seat.

This was not what he'd expected.

She was not what he'd expected.

He wanted her, yes. He'd thought making her spend the week with him was a good idea. But now, he had a sinking feeling that in the next week he was going to get more than he'd bargained for.

"I don't like when my plans are changed." He frowned.

Jade lifted a brow. "I hadn't planned on having dinner with you. Actually, I hadn't planned on ever seeing you again and I most definitely did not plan to spend the week with you. But life is unpredictable. Nothing ever goes exactly as planned."

Her voice was alluring, soft and sultry in the

dimly lit restaurant. His gaze fell to her lips as he listened to her words. Yes, life was unpredictable and most times things didn't go as planned. And if he had his way his plan for a week would last much longer.

Chapter 3

Jade sighed as she sank into the deep cushioned couch in the living room of Linc's penthouse. She was stuffed. Dinner had been magnificent. Giving Linc his due, the restaurant, the casino, the hotel, all of his hard work was apparent. His establishment was every bit as classy and elaborate as his competitors'. But then she'd expected nothing less of him. What did come as a surprise was the fact that he was great with his staff. He knew everyone by their first name, their job title and specifically the shift they worked. And when he spoke to them he seemed genuine. In her experience rich bosses didn't treat their staff like they were personal friends.

Now he moved comfortably through the room. He'd slipped out of his suit jacket and tossed it on the back of an armchair. Under the pretense of resting her eyes she watched him through slit lids. A white dress shirt had never looked so good, but then she'd yet to see him in anything that looked bad. The way the material draped over his broad shoulders and muscled arms had her heart thumping in her chest. Her gaze traveled down to the gold cuff links at his wrists, then toward the gold belt buckle at his waist. And rested there.

Lincoln Donovan was a well-built man. She could not only see that but had the memory of it permanently emblazed on her brain. The thought of him inside her again made her mouth water. Their one night together had been beyond anything she'd ever experienced since then. As far as initiations go she was sure Linc had been the best. He'd been slow and gentle with her as if he'd already known her inexperienced status. There wasn't a part of her body his hands hadn't explored. And it had happened more than once. After the first time he'd continued to lavish her body with attention throughout the night. She thought she'd died and gone to heaven. Until she woke the next morning, alone.

That single thought had her sitting upright on the couch, which was difficult because the cushions were so deep and so soft that keeping her balance was almost impossible.

Maybe if she hadn't been nursing a crush on him since the first time seeing him one year prior to the night they'd spent together, she wouldn't have been devastated when he left. And maybe if she hadn't been filled with silly romantic notions that she would defy her bad luck and fall madly in love with a man who loved her back, she wouldn't have cried for the duration of that next day.

"Do you want a drink?" he asked, startling her from her thoughts.

"No." She wanted to stand up, to go to whatever room she'd be sleeping in, and break this connection they still seemed to have. She wanted to get away from him, plain and simple. But she couldn't get out of the damned chair. She struggled to stand, bracing her hands on the cushions at her sides and attempting to lift herself up.

In seconds he was there, his hands going beneath her arms, pulling her to a standing position, parallel with his tall, rigid form. She sucked in a breath, looked up at him, then to the side. Staring into his eyes was deadly. It made her feel vulnerable, too open for his assault. "I'm ready for bed."

His hands remained on her, his thumbs grazing the side curve of her breasts. Heat spread through her rapidly with waves of desire building steadily. Her knees wobbled and her nipples hardened— damned traitorous body of hers. He was the enemy. He'd hurt her once, no way was he going to do it again.

She tried to move out of his grasp but he held firm. "There's a big bed in the master suite," he said seductively.

He pulled her closer to him until his burgeoning erection was positioned between her thighs. His message was very clear. "I'm ready to go to sleep," she corrected her earlier declaration.

"I know just how to put you to sleep."

Jade's breath caught in her throat. How could one man's touch erase all intelligent thought from her mind? It hadn't been this way with Charles. Then again, she and Charles never shared an active sex life. Come to think of it sex had never been the same for her since that first time with Linc, hence the reason she didn't indulge as much as the average twenty-eight-year-old. Still, she was determined not to indulge with Lincoln Donovan again.

She pressed her palms against his chest and tried to push him away. That in itself was a mistake. She loved the feel of his rigid muscles beneath her hands and reflexively moved them over his pectorals, to his broad shoulders and down those hard biceps. "I don't need you to help me sleep," she whispered in a voice that didn't sound like her own.

He exuded strength, masculinity and pure unadulterated sex appeal and she wanted him. She didn't want to, but it was undeniable. She could accept lust but she didn't have to act on it. She wouldn't act on it.

Linc's pulse raced. Had he ever wanted a woman so badly before? Blood pumped fiercely to his groin until his erection strained against his zipper. He pressed into her center again marveling at how perfectly they fit. Her breasts rubbed against his chest and she was touching him. Damn, her hands on his arms of all places were even driving him wild. Each time her fingers flexed over his taut skin he felt the urge to lift her dress and thrust himself inside her grow stronger. She was trying to tell him that she didn't want him, he could hear it in her voice. But her body was telling him something different.

He stared at her mouth. Propelled by need he leaned down and captured her lips. His mind was full of her as his tongue slid seductively over her closed lips. Her lids fluttered and he drew her bottom lip into his mouth and sucked. Her fingers clenched on his arms. She wanted him as much as he wanted her. Heat raced through his loins and he nipped her lip. She whimpered and he suckled the spot gently. Her taste was simply intoxicating, filling him with something he was sure he'd never felt before.

His tongue plunged inside seeking hers then stroking, suckling and mingling. Her arms went around his neck, pulling him down closer, opening her mouth, taking his tongue and twirling it against her own. Linc closed his eyes to the sensations, the room beginning to slowly spin out of control. Desperation spread through his body like a disease. He could not get enough of her. His hands moved to her back, down to her bottom where he cupped the voluptuous mounds, pressing her center firmly into his erection. Her legs parted with the movement and he moaned deeply into her mouth.

Hot and wet, the kiss continued deepening until his hands finally slipped to the hem of her dress. Fiercely he jerked on the material, pulling it up to her waist. As if following an unknown signal his hand grazed the rim of her panties. Deft fingers pushed the material aside, slipping into her dewy folds.

What had started as a way to get out of a debt was quickly turning into a disaster in the making.

She loved kissing him, loved the feel of his hot mouth on hers. But then he'd touched her there and was now touching her even more. Intimate strokes between her legs were like a beacon in Jade's head and she summoned all the strength she had to wrench herself out of his arms and step away. Breathless from the kiss and thoroughly confused from the emotions he'd aroused, she turned her back to him and tried to regain her composure.

Long seconds ticked by in the silent, sexually charged atmosphere and she wondered briefly what he was thinking, then decided that she didn't care. This was business. There was no room for her feelings to get involved, not with this man, not with any man again. She turned back to find him staring at her, hands fisted at his sides. His eyes were dark with desire, his chest heaving.

It didn't matter. She was his employee for one week. She had to make her stand now or she'd lose before the game had even begun.

"I will sleep alone."

Never, in all his thirty-two years had Linc entertained the idea of forcing a woman to do his bidding. That thought alone caused him to tremble and hesitate. He wanted her fiercely, could imagine his erection slipping inside of her the way his finger almost had. Dragging a hand down his face he inhaled her essence, felt his gut clench and swore. "We made a deal."

Jade squared her shoulders and stared at him, fighting the urge to give him what they both desperately wanted. "The deal was for a date for the week. When I sleep with a man, it's on my terms, my decision. It's not a part of a job." She walked out of the room slowly enough for him to stop her if he wanted to although she knew he wouldn't.

Linc might be arrogant and he might be domineering but—even though she'd accused him of it—he was not cruel. He wouldn't force her to do something she didn't want to do. He'd proved that the night of the party. He hadn't done anything to her without her express permission first even though they'd both been drinking. No, if she slept with Lincoln Donovan again, business or not, it would be because she wanted to. And because her heart still hammered in her chest, her lips still tingled from his kiss, her center still pulsed from his touch, that thought alone frightened her.

Linc awoke the next morning in the master suite. Alone. He hadn't taken a cold shower in years, but last night after she'd almost kissed the wits out of him then left him standing there panting like a dog in heat he'd had no other choice.

He'd lain awake for hours trying to get her out of his mind, trying to erase the feel of her body against his, the scent of her desire out of his head, that look of fear he'd glimpsed seconds after she'd pulled away. Another hour was spent kicking himself for moving so fast. They hadn't been together in eight years. It was foolish of him to instantly try and pick up where they'd left off. Because he hadn't stuck around he'd never known how she'd felt about that night they'd spent together. He'd immediately moved out of the dorm, returning to campus only to take his remaining classes. He hadn't wanted to bump into her again.

Had she been hurt by his leaving?

He doubted that. A week later he'd had a close call when leaving the campus library later than usual one night. He'd seen her in the arms of another man smiling happily up at him as they walked. No, Jade Vincent was not pining over him at all. He silently thanked his instincts and made an even more concerted effort to never see her again.

In the morning he faced the fact that she'd probably been right to stop them. This was about money for her. Every woman's bottom line was money where he was concerned. She'd agreed to be his date, not to sleep with him. As she'd made perfectly clear last night, if she slept with him it would be because she wanted to.

He amended that statement. *When* she slept with him, it would definitely be because she wanted to. He wouldn't have it any other way. As far as her terms, well, he wasn't willing to think about them right now.

In an hour they would leave for his parents' house. That thought soothed him a bit. Fifteen years ago Henry Donovan had acquired a stretch of land in the Pahranagat Valley, just ninety miles northeast of Las Vegas. Initially he was going to sell it until his wife had seen it and fallen in love with the rich scenery. Henry had had a mansion built there instead and about five years ago added horse breeding to his repertoire.

Linc continued to think of his parents and of the forty years they'd been together. Henry and Beverly were the epitome of love and happiness. Funny how their sons avoided the same things like the plague. But lately Beverly had begun hinting at the fact that she had no grandchildren and that her sons were sorely disappointing her. Sure, she loved them, would do anything for them, but she wanted them married and settled. It was that simple. At least in her mind it was. Linc knew differently.

In the past months he'd grown tired of the women his mother not so discreetly sent his way. They simply didn't appeal to him on a long-term level. Up until a week or so ago he hadn't even thought he wanted someone on a long-term level. While he still wasn't entertaining thoughts of marriage, he had begun to think that his discontent centered around his lackluster personal life.

His mother would love to hear that and Linc had no doubt she would have more than enough women at the house this week to perk up that personal life of his. She had a surprise coming.

The first half hour of their ride passed in virtual silence after a brief breakfast of fruit and coffee. Jade's stomach growled and she coughed to muffle the sound. Linc had offered to order a full meal but she'd been stubborn, and anxious to get this show on the road. She'd barely slept last night and was having second thoughts about this deal with him. Maybe she would have been better off applying for a personal loan herself to pay Noelle's debt. But she had enough overhead right now. Another bill wasn't the answer.

With a sigh she decided she'd have to find some way to deal with this attraction to Linc and the business deal they'd struck. He fully expected her to sleep with him. She had no intention of getting her feelings tangled up in him again. Linc had broken her heart once and she wasn't about to give him the opportunity to do it again.

Last night she'd wondered how she considered

the one-night stand with Linc a lost relationship while her six-month engagement to Charles was written off as a fatal mistake. She'd liked Charles well enough—Grammy had liked him more—but she had to admit to feeling a small sense of relief when she opened his e-mail that fateful morning. There was no love lost where Charles was concerned. Anger was more likely the emotion of choice when she thought of him. Her fists clenched at the memory. If she ever saw Charles again she'd...

Linc reached over, touched her hands, slowly pulling her fingers out as he stared at her. "What are you thinking about over there?"

"Huh? Oh, nothing. I wasn't thinking about anything," she said, embarrassed that he'd obviously been watching her.

"It must have been something. You were about to draw your own blood."

She shrugged. "Just something that's better left in the past."

"Did somebody hurt you?"

Jade stared at him blankly then quickly turned away. "No. Nobody hurt me."

"They made you angry?"

She opened her mouth to speak then clamped it shut again. Why did he care either way? "Let's just say my life's been full of lessons learned."

He folded her hand in his and Jade felt the familiar heat stirring inside.

"I'd be interested in hearing about those lessons." He smiled and then held up a hand to stop her when she would have spoken. "But for now I'll settle for hearing about what you've been doing for the past eight years."

Making one mistake after another, pining for you, losing a fortune... Where should she start? Jade shifted in the seat. What was it about him that made her want to scream one minute and melt into his arms the next? At any rate, telling him about her past mistakes was definitely out of the question. Switching the subject would be better. "I have a better idea. Why don't you give me the rundown on your family? Since I'll be spending a week with them I should probably know some basics."

Linc gave her a half smile. She hadn't admitted it but he was sure there was someone in her past who she was still pretty angry with and he was willing to bet the person was a man. He looked into warm hazel eyes and wanted instinctively to protect her from all hurt and harm. She had secrets, ones that caused her great pain. He wondered how long it would take her to tell him, then decided it didn't really matter. At least he didn't want it to.

"I am the oldest of three boys. I have two brothers—Trent and Adam. Trent's an ex-Navy Seal and Adam's into real estate. My parents, Henry and Beverly, have been married for forty years and will invite every living member of the Donovan family to the house this week to help them celebrate."

"Hmm," she sighed. When her mother had died it had been just her, Noelle and Grammy. She'd always longed for a big family. "What do your parents do?"

Linc chuckled. "Not much of anything anymore. My father was a third generation rich kid, following in his father's footsteps. He ran the family oil company for about twenty years before deciding to retire. Now he finds hobbies. For a few years he was a racing sponsor, then he dabbled in marine biology and right now he's into horse breeding."

"He sounds like an interesting man," Jade said wistfully.

"He is. Mom comes from money. Her father was an oil tycoon. Now she has her charities and her clubs. But her main job as of late seems to be finding a wife for me."

Jade's heart skipped a beat. "A wife?"

His thumb continued to move absently over the back of her hand. "Yeah, she's pretty focused on the task." Then he looked at her. "That's why I needed you this week."

"I don't understand."

"I don't need my mother to find me a wife. My life is just fine as it is but Mom is stuck on the idea that I need a wife and kids to make me complete. She'll have a bunch of women that she believes are good enough for me at the house this week trying to make a match. With you along as my date, she'll have to back off. Appearances are everything to her. She'd never embarrass you or me by pushing another woman on me in your presence."

She blinked, appearing to be digesting his words. "So my purpose is to stand in the way of your finding the love of your life."

"There is no love of my life. I'm just a man, doing man things."

"Oh," she said simply, not completely sure how she felt about those "man things."

Mario drove up to black gates and pressed a combination into the security box to gain entrance. Jade's attention shifted to her surroundings. It looked like Southfork Ranch, from the hit series *Dallas,* had been thrust into the twenty-first century. Lush green lawns surrounded a huge fountain that sat in the middle of a circular driveway. Just beyond the fountain was a house that looked like it would easily accommodate a hundred or so residents. An all-brick structure with black shutters and white columns sat comfortably amidst huge trees and an awesome blue sky. It was picturesque to say the least.

Before she had a chance to get over the splendor her door opened and Mario was reaching inside for her hand. Linc had released her other hand and was scooting along the seat behind her. He was so close now she could smell his cologne mixed with the fresh spring breeze coming in from the outside. Taking Mario's lead she stepped out of the car onto the gravelly walkway and immediately looked around again.

Linc stepped out behind her placing a hand at the small of her back. "I'll give you a tour then we'll go in and meet my parents. I'm not sure if Trent and Adam are here yet."

Jade was silent, still trying to take in her surroundings and the fact that Linc was close and touching her again. There was a light breeze and blooms from a nearby tree scattered about the ground just as the front door to the house opened and a couple stepped out.

The woman was beautiful, her hair perfectly styled, her summer suit a flattering shade of mint green. The man wore slacks and a polo shirt. He looked just like Linc except his hair had started to thin on the top, but the build and coloring were exactly the same. She suspected they were in their early sixties but they both appeared as youthful and healthy as twenty-year-olds. They smiled in her direction and she dutifully smiled back.

"Lincoln, darling," the woman cooed. "We were wondering when you'd get here." Coming up on tiptoes the woman hugged him.

Jade watched as Linc embraced her, feeling the love between mother and son.

"Good morning, Mom. I told you I'd be driving up this morning."

"I know, but you could have come yesterday like your brothers," she said, stepping aside so that Linc could likewise hug his father.

"Son, it's good to see you." The older man clapped Linc's back as they embraced.

Jade felt out of place and took a step back to give them time for their mini reunion. Just as she was moving out of the way the woman grabbed her hand. "And who, might I ask, is this?"

Jade froze. Linc said that appearances were everything to his mother. She wondered how the woman would feel about her being here. She wasn't exactly a socialite, although she knew how to act in front of company, compliments of Grammy's upbringing. She hadn't noticed Linc returning to her side until his hand snaked around her waist. She should have pulled away, should have left him and this silly charade and returned to her normal, bad-luck life. Considering that wasn't an option at this point she simply smiled and leaned closer to him.

"It's very nice to meet you both," she managed in a nervous voice. "Happy anniversary." Jade was beyond nervous but prayed it didn't show. She'd never met a man's parents before. Charles's parents traveled a lot, or so he'd said. Now she figured any- and everything that man had told her had most likely been a lie.

Beverly looked from her son back to Jade with undeniable questions in her eyes. Still holding Jade's hand she surveyed her yet again. Jade didn't know whether she'd made the right choice of clothes this morning but she felt certain that Beverly was surmising that very point.

"Please excuse me for staring, but Lincoln has never brought a young lady home to meet us before. I'm a little surprised," she said.

Mrs. Donovan was more than a little surprised but Jade decided that was not her problem. She only needed to be polite, to get through the next seven days and then she'd never have to deal with any of the Donovans again. "I look forward to spending the week helping you and your husband celebrate."

"Oh, dear, we have so much planned. You are simply going to enjoy yourself. Now come along. Let me give you a tour and we can get to know each other a little. Lincoln is so rude, he's never even mentioned you."

I'm sure he hasn't, Jade thought, tossing Linc a baleful look. He hadn't said she'd be spending time *alone* with his mother. What was she supposed to say when they were alone? She prayed the woman didn't ask her questions about her relationship with Linc. Jade didn't like lying—omitting certain parts of the truth was one thing, but outright lying about a nonexistent relationship with a man who only had a passing interest in her was crossing the line. But before another word could be said Beverly had shuffled her off leaving Linc and Henry alone. They both looked on as the women departed.

"Pretty good-looking woman," Henry said.

Linc grinned. "You've been with her for forty years and you're just realizing that."

Henry chuckled. "I know *my* woman's fine. I was talking about yours."

His woman? Jade was *not* his woman. Then he corrected himself. She was for the week at least.

Chapter 4

Jade walked into the huge dining room and all talking ceased. She'd toured the estate with Mrs. Donovan before being led to her room—the room she and Linc were expected to share in the east wing of the house—and directed to wash and change for lunch. She'd never changed for meals before but figured now was not the time to bring that point to Mrs. Donovan's attention.

The woman was the epitome of style and grace. With a slim figure and knowing eyes, Mrs. Donovan had talked of general things like education and career goals but Jade knew she'd been sizing her up. Which was exactly what Jade herself was doing. A little self-evaluation never hurt. As a result, she'd come to the conclusion that she was definitely not in Linc's league.

These people had ten cars in their garage, a tennis court, a golf course, an indoor and outdoor pool and a solarium. Oh, and she hadn't even mentioned the stables, which were magnificent by the way. She'd ridden a horse once when she was a little girl and had instantly fallen in love with the chocolate pony that had taken her around in circles. But then she'd never given another thought to riding a horse since that day, no matter how much she'd enjoyed it. That just went to show you what type of people she was dealing with.

Mrs. Donovan informed her that she rode every day when she could, that it was like an obsession to her and her husband. In Jade's average, but basically happy, life, even as the owner of a spa, she never anticipated owning horses or a stable that she could walk to at any time to ride.

But this was their life. A life that she was painfully aware she'd never fit into. Jade decided not to think about their difference in social status anymore. There would be no misguided daydreams about her presence in Linc's life this time. Accordingly, what Mrs. Donovan thought of her was no big deal. Or at least it shouldn't be.

She'd changed into another pair of slacks and a silky halter top and prayed that this would be appropriate. Actually, she prayed that this would be the quickest week of her life.

"That's a beautiful color on you, Jade." Mrs. Donovan motioned for her to take the seat left empty to the right of her when she'd finally made it downstairs. Mrs. Donovan sat at one end of the long oak table while her husband sat at the opposite end. The brothers, Adam and Trent, sat on either side leaving two chairs, one to the right and one to the left of their mother. Presumably those seats were for her and Linc, who was nowhere to be found.

"Thank you," Jade said with a wavering smile. She was here as Linc's date, as his convenient arm piece for the week, so why was she at this family luncheon and he wasn't? "Is Linc coming?"

"We were just about to ask you the same thing," Trent commented dryly.

Noting his tone, but deciding to dismiss it, Jade took her seat and reached for the napkin centered on her plate. "Nope. I haven't seen him since we arrived."

Mr. Donovan, who had been staring at her since the moment she'd walked in, took a sip from his glass then spoke. "He's in the den making a few calls."

"He's working? He hasn't eaten anything all day," Jade exclaimed.

"He's a big boy. I'm sure he knows when it's time to eat." This was from Trent, who, Jade noted again, spoke to her in clipped tones. What the hell was up with him?

"Still, he should join us," Mrs. Donovan interrupted.

Mr. Donovan shook his head. "Let him get his work done now. You know how important it is to him. Then he'll be free for the rest of the week."

A small woman dressed in a neat gray-and-white uniform had slipped quietly through a door at the back of the room. She carried a tray and proceeded to stop in front of each of them placing a bowl before them. Jade inhaled and thought she'd died and gone to heaven. She loved crab soup but hadn't eaten it since Grammy died. Without another word she picked up her spoon and dug in. It was a few minutes before she realized she was the only one eating.

Heat infused her cheeks. She wasn't slurping nor had she spilled any on the gorgeous linen tablecloth, so why was everybody staring at her...again? She looked around and noted that the nicely dressed server was placing a plate laden with sandwiches in the center of the table. So it was to be a soup and sandwich meal? Well, she could eat the sandwich later, she thought and continued happily with her soup.

"So what do you do, Jade?" Adam smiled at her.

Jade found herself smiling back. Adam was the youngest of the Donovan men; his laughing brown eyes and dimpled cheeks said he was also the happiest. He eagerly lifted not one, not two, but three half-sandwich portions from the serving tray and dropped them onto the plate beside his soup bowl. Adam was built quite nicely. As a matter of fact all three of the Donovan brothers were exceptionally handsome and well built. But to Jade, none of them quite measured up to Linc. Still, Adam possessed the kind of carefree attitude Jade was normally attracted to. Trent, on the other hand, needed to take a chill pill.

"I'm a licensed massage therapist." She didn't mention the fact that she owned her own spa because that seemed to pale in comparison to what the Donovans were used to as a way to make a living.

"She also graduated from Harvard. That's where she and Lincoln met," Mrs. Donovan added.

"So you've known Linc for about eight or nine years now?"

Leveling her gaze at Trent, the middle child, the one with the cool dark eyes and a strong jaw, she tried to read his expression. If she didn't know better she'd think he was purposefully goading her. Instead she was slightly intrigued by this instant dislike he directed toward her. "Yes. But we haven't seen each other in quite some time."

"And you picked now to show up?"

"Actually, I didn't pick anything. I went to the Gramercy for some R&R. My grandmother passed away almost a year ago and I needed to get out and do something with myself. I had no idea that Linc owned the Gramercy." Part truth was just as good as total honesty, she reminded herself.

"But you were happy to find out weren't you?"

"Trent, that's enough," Mr. Donovan stated adamantly.

So the lion had decided to bare his teeth after all. Jade never backed down from a battle. It would do Trent good to find this out now. "I was not looking for your brother, who I knew from the moment I met him eight years ago would be successful. So to answer your question, yes. It was good to see Linc again and yes, I was proud of what he'd accomplished with his life." She took a deep breath and continued to stare at Trent. "And no, the fact that he owns a casino did not register dollar signs in my mind. I have my own education and ambition and I don't need to ride on anybody's coattails."

Adam grinned. "Score one for Jade and a whopping goose egg for Trent."

Mr. Donovan rolled his eyes.

Mrs. Donovan wiped her hands on her napkin. "That's enough, Trent. Jade is Lincoln's guest and we will be nothing but polite to her. It's good to see Lincoln with someone. He appears happy."

Jade turned at the woman's words. Did he appear happy? She couldn't tell. But then it didn't matter. Lifting her spoon to her mouth again Jade silently chanted "business, not pleasure," over and over again.

The meal was soon over and even though Trent seemed to question her more than others Jade found that she enjoyed herself. Mr. Donovan was quite the comedian once he managed to get a word in between his wife and his youngest son. Adam was hands down her favorite Donovan—in the room, that is. With his laughing eyes and easy personality he was a stark contrast to Trent's serious, almost suspicious nature.

But neither of them measured up to Linc. Throughout the meal she found her thoughts constantly returning to him. His presence did something to her, something other than annoy her with memories, something she wasn't quite willing to examine just yet. Besides, she wanted to do her job to the best of her ability; dismissing the five-thousand-dollar debt was all that mattered.

Her heels clicked on the hardwood floors in the foyer of the Donovan home. She paused in the living room to examine all the family photos strewn about. They seemed so happy, so complete. On her mantel in her apartment she had a photo of her, Noelle and her mother when she was six and her, Grammy and Noelle when she'd graduated from Harvard. Emptiness settled over her as she traced a hand along one silver-trimmed frame.

Quickly regaining her senses she left the beautifully decorated room in search of the den and Linc. He was sitting in a sage-green high-backed chair. This room was warm, more inviting than any of the others in the house. With its coppery wallpaper and forest-green carpet, the lighter green furniture looked comfortable and relaxing. Coming farther in the room she realized he was on the speakerphone so when she would normally have immediately spoken, this time she remained quiet. Going to the couch she sat, crossing one leg over the other, watching him as he flipped through a folder and talked in that smooth, commanding voice that sent pleasurable chills down her spine.

He still wore the slacks and polo shirt he'd worn since this morning, his thick biceps straining just a bit against the rim of his sleeves. She sucked in a breath as his broad chest moved rhythmically while he spoke. Confidence oozed from his every pore and she couldn't help but admire him. He was a success. He ran a lucrative business he seemed to enjoy. He had it all. She not only admired him, she envied him. These were the things she wanted. The things that always seemed just out of her reach.

Linc felt her presence. The moment she'd walked into that room, he'd known, his whole body becoming alert. She sat across from him now looking like she had a lot on her mind. Lines knotted her forehead and caused him to frown. The urge to cure whatever it was that ailed her was great. That bothered him, so he shifted to thoughts he more easily understood—the physical pull between them.

She'd changed clothes, the pants clinging to her hips a little more than the ones she'd had on earlier and the deep green color of the top highlighting her hazel eyes, its thin straps drawing his attention immediately to the honey-toned skin of her bare shoulders and inevitably the plump roundness of her breasts. He shifted in the chair, his erection making it harder to sit still.

She licked her lips and he almost expired right then and there. He'd have to cut this phone call short or risk embarrassing himself with his colleague. "So I'll give you a call in the morning and we can go over the rest of the figures," he said in closing.

He'd long since given up looking at the papers in the folder and was now solely focused on the minx across from him. With her legs crossed she dangled one sandal-clad foot in the air. The heels were spiked, at least four inches high, and he could imagine how they emphasized those long, gorgeous legs of hers. The man on the phone's voice resonated throughout the room but Linc had no idea what he'd said. Standing on less than stable legs he went to the desk and said quickly, "Yes, I'll call you in the morning." Before the man could respond he'd switched off the speaker-phone and went to face her.

Without another word he reached for her hands and hefted her to her feet. Her breasts—to his immense delight—made instant contact with his chest as his hands moved around her waist. "Did you come in here to deliberately tempt me?" he asked in a low voice.

"No. I came in here to tell you that your family expects you to participate in the week's events, not work the entire time."

He raised a brow. "Did you miss me?"

She moved out of his embrace. "You wish."

He watched her walk away and stop in front of

the window. "They're about to play golf," she said as she turned to face him again.

"I don't play golf."

He managed a smile, relief at the disappearance of the lines in her forehead spreading through him. He still couldn't believe she was actually here with him. Last night, he'd wondered why she'd really agreed to this week. That question had led to several more, like what she did for a living.

"Then what do you do? For fun, I mean," she continued.

"We've all been asking ourselves that question for years now." Adam chuckled as he entered and walked across the room idly swinging a golf club.

Both Linc and Jade acknowledged the intruder, Linc with a scowl and Jade suppressing a grin. "Shouldn't you be out on the course?" Linc asked, eyeing his brother's attire.

"Shouldn't you?" Adam added teasingly.

"That's what I was trying to tell him," Jade interrupted. "Your father said some of his friends were coming by to play. Your mother had some sort of last-minute meeting to attend but suggested that I take a swim."

Linc thrust his hands in his pockets in an attempt to hide his growing arousal. The mere thought of Jade's seductive body, wet and barely clad, had his mouth watering. He could just imagine licking each droplet from her moist skin, exploring her completely as he'd done before. It had been a long time yet he'd never forgotten her sweetness.

He cleared his throat. "I don't play golf."

"But you do ride," Adam said with a devilish grin. "Horses, I mean. You love to ride...horses, right, Linc?"

Linc hadn't missed his brother's crass remark and frowned as it appeared Jade hadn't, either. "I have work to do."

"I'd love to go riding," Jade quickly added.

She folded her arms behind her back, her breasts jutting forward as she toyed with her bottom lip again. Did she have any idea how sexy that was? How when her tongue grazed that plump bottom lip he simply wanted to ravish her? How the sight of her breasts being offered, albeit unknowingly, spiked his blood pressure? No, she didn't know. He was just getting used to the re-alization himself. He desperately wanted to get her in his bed.

Still, he wasn't so lust-filled that he missed the light in her eyes when she spoke of riding. He decided instantly that he liked that light in her eyes and would do whatever he could to keep it there. "Go change. I'll meet you at the stables."

"Great! Thanks for the suggestion, Adam." Planting an impromptu kiss on Adam's cheek she turned and made her way out of the room.

Linc went straight to the bar and felt his brother's elated glare on his back as he did. "Go ahead and say it." He picked up a glass and poured a finger of brandy then drank it down and poured another.

"Say what?" Adam chuckled. He still held his golf club but had now wandered over to the bar to take a seat on a stool. "That it's a little early in the afternoon for drinks?"

Linc scowled. He was disturbed by Adam's intrusion and a little agitated that Jade had readily kissed Adam but couldn't wait to get out of his arms. But mostly he was grumpy because he was horny as hell and couldn't seem to scratch his itch no matter how close she was.

Still grinning Adam twirled the golf club again. "So how did you get her to agree to this week of celebration on the Donovan estate?" he asked.

"What do you mean?" The last thing Linc wanted to do was tell his brother he'd paid for a date. "I asked her to come."

"And because you're the legendary Lincoln Donovan she came?"

Linc shrugged. "You know how I do things."

"Yeah, I do. But I just don't see that working with a woman like Jade."

"What's that supposed to mean? A woman like Jade? What kind of woman is she, Adam?"

"I don't know, she just seems cool, like she has a mind of her own. Did you know she was a masseuse?"

No, he didn't know, and the fact that Adam did, didn't sit well with him. "Look, this is just an arrangement for the week. There's no need for me to get all into her personal life because by Sunday morning she'll be on her way and I'll be on mine." He said the words but felt a sudden jolt at the fact that it might be true.

Adam stood and strolled leisurely toward the door. "I wonder though, how a man could have a woman like that and let her walk away.'

"I don't keep women, Adam. You know that." Everybody knew that, he thought dismally. But what if he were different? What if he did keep women? Would he keep Jade?

Adam turned briefly. "Yeah, I know. The Triple Threat Brothers stand alone."

Linc frowned then filled his glass again. "I'll drink to that," he said, lifting the glass in his brother's direction before downing its contents.

Was it just her or did the sun shine extra bright today?

Jade inhaled deeply letting the not-so-fresh air

fill her lungs. She stood in front of the stables watching while the stable boy saddled a caramel-colored mare for her. Linc saddled his own horse. She stared as the muscles in his back rippled and bulged with his motions. The horse stood perfectly still as if he knew that Lincoln would tolerate nothing less.

That's how it was with Linc. She noticed that everyone around him seemed to operate on command, not doing or saying anything that he hadn't personally requested for fear of what his reaction might be. The stable boy hadn't made any attempt to retrieve Linc's horse or saddle him for that matter. In fact, the young man had waited patiently for Linc to instruct him as to which horse she would ride.

"Saddle up Lily. She's mild tempered," Linc had finally instructed.

Jade bristled at the comment. "Does that mean you think I need a mild-tempered horse? I'll have you know that I've ridden a horse before."

He'd given her a curious look, one that was becoming quite familiar to her. One that made her wonder what he was thinking. "You've never ridden in this terrain and you've never ridden prize horses."

"Are you afraid I'll hurt your precious horse?" she asked sarcastically.

What he said next was a complete surprise.

"I'm more afraid of what will happen if they decide to hurt you."

That hadn't sounded like the Linc she knew so she'd been at a loss for words.

Linc didn't seem to notice as he lifted a leg to swing effortlessly into his own saddle. She had to crane her neck to look up at him and wished she hadn't bothered at all. He was beautiful. They were beautiful together. Lincoln dressed in black jeans and a black T-shirt, his dark complexion framed by the golden sunlight and the majestic ebony creature he sat astride. That horse was made just for him, with a huge build and its shiny coat that said he was well taken care of. It exuded the same power that oozed from Linc. For a brief moment she wondered...just imagined what it would feel like to be so perfectly matched with someone that way.

"Chad, help her up," he directed the stable boy.

Tearing her gaze from him with a heaviness in her chest she couldn't explain Jade looked at Chad. "I can do it myself."

Chad looked from her to Linc, clearly unsure of what to do next. Neither man moved or said a word as she stuck a foot in the stirrup. She grabbed hold of the reins and attempted to hoist herself up as she'd watched Linc do just moments before.

Her thigh slid unceremoniously down the back of the horse.

Okay, so she wasn't smooth enough to get it right the first time, but that was no reason to quit. She tried again…and again until she felt hands go around her waist. Looking over her shoulder she confirmed that it was Linc although the heat soaring through her body had already alerted her to that fact.

"Don't be so stubborn," he said, his warm breath brushing over her ear. He lifted her effortlessly and placed her in the saddle.

Again, she was speechless.

Linc mounted his horse again and trotted past her slowly. Her mare began a slow trot and she frowned at his retreating back. "I am not stubborn."

Jade's mood was sour. And she didn't know why. Okay, she had an idea why. For eight years she'd had only the memory of Linc. And that memory was of a careless, selfish coward. That memory was easy to live with.

In the last two days she'd begun to see something else. Something that she despised even more. He was a gentleman. He obviously loved his family. And he wasn't totally careless. These things were much harder to swallow.

In fact, there was no use in listing Linc's good points. They didn't matter. Nothing mattered but the fact that by the end of this week that debt would be cleared. She had to focus on only that.

They'd been riding for almost a half hour in complete silence. Linc didn't take his horse above a mild canter and when she'd tried to go beyond that he'd quickly caught up with her and grabbed her reins. Now she had no choice but to stay right beside him as he only allowed a slight berth between them. Nevertheless, the scenery was magnificent. While Nevada is known for its steamy deserts, the Donovans' land was an endless stretch of emerald green. Acres and acres of rolling lushness that boasted the simple life, a life of rest and relaxation personified.

She reveled in that for a while, remembering how Grammy always wanted to live in the country. She had planned to buy her a house just as soon as the spa was doing well. After the hefty inheritance Grammy had left for her, Jade wondered why her grandmother hadn't simply bought her country home herself before she died. Thoughts of Grammy had her feeling nostalgic and she glanced at Linc.

He looked tense, as if something weighed heavily on his mind. She wondered if he was regretting asking her to come. He could have easily found another date. Why he'd asked her to do this was a mystery. This made her question, for the millionth time, what had happened eight years ago. Why had he approached her and asked her to accompany him to his room? Even then he could have had his choice of girls. They were from different worlds. She was sure he'd known that then just as he knew it now.

"Why did you leave?" she asked spontaneously.

"What?" He looked at her with a baffled expression.

"That night in your dorm. Why did you leave without saying goodbye? I mean, you could have stayed. It was your room." Although he held the reins she nervously twisted her fingers around the leather strap of the saddle. Business deal or not they had a past and she felt like she deserved an answer. Whatever he said now wouldn't change what happened but she would finally be able to reconcile with it.

He paused another minute. "It doesn't matter. It's in the past."

"It does matter. We were both consenting adults. I would think that earned me some level of respect."

He didn't look at her but spoke quietly. "It wasn't what you thought."

"Then tell me what it was. I gave myself to you freely. If you didn't want me you should have been man enough to stick around and say that."

"I wanted you…" His words trailed off.

"Just not for keeps." The admission hurt her more than she'd anticipated. Why, after all this time, was the pain still so fresh and so strong? She turned away from him then looked toward the golf course just beyond the house.

Linc turned down an incline that led into a cluster of trees, yanking on the straps as he pulled her horse along. "I can't go back and change what I did."

"I know," she said sadly, wishing they could both go back and make different decisions.

He took a deep breath and looked as if he were contemplating what to say next. "I didn't want a relationship," he said in a quiet tone. "I had plans."

His dark eyes were nondescript. There was something strangely consuming about his response, about the quick shift in direction, the hint of emotion he'd let slip. Was he angry with her or with himself? "I don't recall asking you to marry me, Linc."

He let out a deep breath and dropped her reins as they came to a small creek. Both horses bowed their heads to drink. Linc glanced up at the sky, then toward the trees. He didn't speak and neither did she. Around them birds chirped and the light rustle of water soothed even as emotions ran hot and swift between them.

"I'm sure you've heard the rumors that I'm not marriage material," he began quietly. "I never have been. I'm self-centered and ambitious. Those things keep me from actively participating in a healthy relationship."

"Only you can keep yourself from being in a relationship. Being self-centered and ambitious aren't totally bad traits. I mean, without them you wouldn't be where you are today."

He looked at her quizzically. "I never thought of being in a relationship with a woman, especially not back then."

Jade shrugged. "I had no idea what I wanted out of life eight years ago." Again a partial truth. She'd known without a doubt that she wanted to be with him.

Silence hung between them again.

"Do you have regrets?" she asked quietly.

"I don't regret what we shared together."

Jade turned away from him, her horse taking a small step as she nudged the reins from his hands. A part of him wanted to go to her, to tell her the things he'd held back. But how could he explain that she'd scared him, that the intense emotions he'd felt as they'd lain together that night had threatened his entire future. Clenching his fists at his sides he swore under his breath. He hadn't meant to hurt her and yet realized that's exactly what he'd done. He'd called it protecting her, protecting them both from the ultimate disappointment. Instead he'd made an awful mistake.

A mistake he badly wanted to rectify now. He would take this week to make it up to her, to reassure her that he had wanted her then but their timing was wrong. Linc wondered if now was any better.

He was about to move toward her to calm the tension now lingering between them when he felt something whiz past his ear and land with a loud splash into the creek. Both horses jumped but he quickly steadied his. Turning in his saddle he realized that Jade hadn't quite handled her mare and was now trying to wrap the reins around her wrists as the mare started an uneasy trot. Linc turned his horse to help her when another object, a golf ball he now realized as he heard a voice yelling "Fore" in the distance, hurtled toward them landing against the hind quarters of Jade's horse. The mare took off into a wild gallop.

Jade's ponytail swayed and bobbed as she was jostled by the horse's erratic running. Linc followed her trying to catch up to the frightened mare. Jade looked like a rag doll being tossed about as the horse tore through the grass up a small hill and around a bend. She was just a few feet away when he saw the reins slip from her hands. Everything shifted to slow motion as fear clawed at Linc's chest.

Time stood still as he watched her body being tossed from the saddle, landing on the ground with a loud thump that had him swearing a blue streak. Pulling on his own reins Linc jumped down before his horse could come to a complete stop and ran to her side. His heart pumped wildly in his chest as he watched her curl up into a ball and whimper in pain. Without another thought he lifted her into his arms and began walking back toward the house.

Jade groaned. "I can walk on my own."

Thankful that she was at least conscious Linc dropped a chaste kiss on her forehead. His own heart still hammered in his chest as the sight of her falling to the ground replayed itself repeatedly in his mind. "You took a bad fall. I'm not letting you go until you're checked out by a doctor."

"I don't need a doctor," she protested.

He ignored her. "You're seeing a doctor."

She looked up at him and rolled her eyes. "I don't need a doctor," she mumbled.

Linc swore. Had he ever known anyone as

stubborn as this woman? With a heated concession he realized he did. Himself.

Looking down at her he said with finality, "It's not an option."

Chapter 5

"Shh." Linc clapped a hand over Jade's mouth and settled her back against the numerous pillows on the bed in their room. He had a private suite in the house, as did his brothers. The doctor had left them just moments before. Thankfully Jade was just bruised and nothing was broken. His heart had only resumed a normal rhythm after the doctor's diagnosis. He'd stood right beside her during the examination ignoring her heated looks. There was a particularly harsh bruise on her upper thigh that bothered him immensely, hence the reason he was going to run her a hot bath. But if she didn't stop fighting him at every turn he was going to hog tie and gag her!

He returned from the bathroom to find that she hadn't gotten up from the bed as he'd fully expected she would, but she had adjusted herself and the pillows so that she was sitting up. Her eyes were still shooting flaming arrows at him. "I am not a child. The doctor said there are no broken bones so there's no reason for me to stay in this bed."

Linc decided it was best not to argue moot points with her. She wouldn't listen anyway. Instead he took purposeful strides toward the bed and pulled down the covers. "Fine, since you are not a child, I'll give you a choice. Either you can undress yourself and get into the tub or I'll do it for you."

Her eyes closed to mere slits as she folded her arms over her chest. "Are you planning to watch?"

He gave a sarcastic grin. "Would it bother you if I did?" Truth be told he was looking forward to seeing her naked again—perhaps that was his secret motive to running her a bath. But she was hurt. In fact, her fall had scared a good five years off his life. He would not take advantage of her now…no matter how tempted he was.

Chin jutting forward and one elegantly arched brow rising, Jade smirked. "Of course not. If it's a show you want, a show you'll get." She slipped her legs from the bed slowly and when her feet hit the floor stood while her eyes remained fixed on his.

She'd changed from that sexy tank top she'd worn to lunch earlier to a fitted V-neck shirt that had been tucked securely in her jeans until the doctor had stripped them from her to inspect the damage. Grabbing the rim of the shirt she pulled it over her head, slowly, so as to draw out every painful second.

Linc's breath caught at the sight of her wearing only her underwear, which was in defiant contrast to the feisty woman standing before him. A subtle, almost virginal, ivory-colored lace bikini and bra set lay against her bronzed skin. Her breasts all but spilling over the rim of the bra, the bikini riding low on her hips, he felt a familiar constriction in his pants. So she wanted to play with fire. Maybe he'd reconsider how hurt she really was.

Arching a brow of his own he asked, "You planning to take a bath in those?" He nodded toward her body. To her credit and his extreme pleasure she did not flinch.

She was stubborn and bold and self-assured, all traits he confessed to possessing himself. He was liking her more and more.

With an agility he didn't see often she reached
behind her back and unclasped her own bra then
let the silky material fall to the floor. High breasts
stood erect, their darkened center drawing his attention. This time, he was the one to flinch. He'd
felt them in his hands, remembered them from
years ago but now seeing them bared before him
rendered him speechless. He took a step closer
and she took one backward. With a finger in the
band of her bikini she pushed the wisp of lace
down over her hips.

His chest constricted, air—something he often
took for granted—leaving the vicinity so that he
was left gasping. She was perfect. From her sleek
shoulders to her graciously rounded breasts. Her
narrow waist spanned out to supple hips, the
triangle of dark hair between her thighs…and then
that bruise. He frowned, reached out to touch her
only to have her push his hand away.

"I'm taking a bath, remember?" And with that
she sashayed into the bathroom, without an ounce
of modesty.

Her heart hammered in her chest as she crossed
the threshold into the bathroom that she could
easily fit her living and dining rooms into. She'd
just performed a striptease for Lincoln Donovan!
She must be out of her mind!

No, she'd been challenged and if there was one thing she never turned down it was a challenge. So she'd undressed herself. Besides, what was the alternative? Having Linc undress her? She was about to go into cardiac arrest now; she would have simmered and spontaneously combusted if he'd put his hands on her!

Oh well, that was over and done with. She'd shocked him speechless, a fact that pleased her immensely. She wasn't used to playing the wanton but found she was thoroughly enjoying it. Linc was very responsive and she toyed with the idea that this would be the ultimate payback for what he'd done to her eight years ago. The thought of revenge brought Charles to mind and how she'd love to repay him for his betrayal. Then she spotted the huge tub and couldn't wait to sink her tired bones into it.

Being thrown from a horse was no joke. Her body hurt all over, bringing to light the fact that she could use more riding practice. A puff of bubbles floated above the chrome moldings of the deep tub and she quickly bent over to turn the water off.

"The view just keeps getting better and better," Linc said in a deep voice.

Jade had used all her composure after the stripping incident so his voice startled her and she slipped on the rim of the tub. As if it had been scripted Linc appeared by her side scooping her naked body into his arms with the pretense of saving her from another fall.

"Funny, you weren't that clumsy a few minutes ago."

Flattening her palms against his chest—against that massive chest that she longed to stroke her tongue over—she tried to push him away. "I wasn't being spied on a few minutes ago."

His features were rigid, his eyes much darker than they had been in the bedroom. His body was like a wall against hers and no matter how much pushing she did against it, it didn't budge. He grunted. "Keep squirming, darling, and your bath is going to grow very cold," he drawled.

Jade suddenly realized that another part of his anatomy was rather hard as well. Her center moistened with the knowledge and she stilled. His erection was pressed against the juncture between her thighs, hard and persistent. "Let me go."

He shook his head slowly. "I'm trying." His voice was strained even as his head lowered toward hers. "Can't you tell I'm trying?"

He was a whisper away, her breasts swelling against him. God, she wanted him to kiss her. Apparently he wanted the same thing. "Put a little more effort into it," she whispered, lifting her lips to his.

Jade's arms went around his neck and she clung to him, hungrily accepting his kiss, ignoring the warning in the back of her head.

Stop him before he goes too far, the faint whisper spoke. Instead her hands tightened at the base of his neck, pulling him closer even as she tilted her head for better access.

He'll hurt you again. Not as long as I'm in control, she answered herself then thrust her tongue deeper into his mouth causing his hands to tighten around her then slip lower to grip her bottom.

Don't trust him. She couldn't trust any man after Charles, least of all a man she had nothing in common with. Still, she melted against him, loving the feel of his commanding lips, his dominating tongue that savored and caressed, retreated and demanded then blurred her senses completely. Instinctively and because she wanted to be as close to him as humanly possible Jade lifted her leg, wrapping her thighs around his waist.

His response was a deep, guttural groan creating a surge of ravenous hunger that would not quickly be appeased. His erection was now dead center with her arousal and she whimpered with the sweet sensations it evoked. That little voice was now lost, to be replaced by the stronger voice that said *take, indulge, enjoy.* She'd dreamed of him for countless nights, remembering his touch, his body, the man. And now she had him back. Sure, it was just for a week, but if right now were any indication, what a wonderful seven days this could be.

She was on fire, her breasts growing heavier by the minute, her essence dampening her core. He sucked her tongue and she thought she would simply die on the spot. He nipped her lip and she moaned. His tongue moved sinuously over her chin, her jawbone, her ear, down her neck. She held on tight for fear she would completely fall apart. Dropping her head back gave him more access and her infinitely more pleasure. His tongue was hot and masterful as it explored her collarbone, her shoulders. Had she ever had her shoulders kissed?

Erotic tingles shot throughout her body and her fingers tensed on his shoulders. His lips hovered just inches above her breasts and he paused, seemed to think about his next action, then returned to her mouth, ravaging her with a brazenly tempting kiss. "More," he grumbled.

And she obliged by holding him tighter, opening her mouth wider, thrusting her tongue quicker. When strong hands squeezed her bottom her blood pressure soared. And when two fingers slipped between her crease to find her creamy center her head fell back and a catlike moan escaped.

All conscious thought fled from her mind and she held her breath waiting for the dam to finally break. She wanted him inside her right now! She prepared to shift, slipping an arm between their bodies until she felt the snap of his jeans and just when she was about to pull them apart...there was a knock at the door.

They paused, hearts beating rapidly against each other. Linc rested his forehead against hers as they tried to regulate their breathing.

"Lincoln? I heard about Jade's fall. Is she all right?"

It was Mrs. Donovan, her voice having the effect of a bucket of cold water being dropped on them.

Linc swore then reluctantly eased her down. "We are not finished," he said in a tone that left no room for argument.

No, she had finally admitted to herself, they weren't finished. Whatever had been between them years ago still lingered at the brink waiting to be set free. Jade only wished she had a better understanding of what it was. She wished, as she had all her life, that her luck wasn't always so bad.

She watched him leave wondering if these same thoughts were going through his head. On shaky legs she turned and as fast as she could—without falling, that is—she stepped into the tub and leaned back against the rim.

He's not the marrying kind. That pesky little voice was back. This time she didn't totally ignore it.

Despite Linc's reservations Jade appeared in the dining room for dinner that night. After her bath he'd watched her take the pain pills the doctor had left for her then ordered her to stay in bed until he returned. He had some calls to make and didn't want to disturb her rest by making them in the room.

Who was he kidding? He needed to get away from her before he forgot that she was recovering from a pretty nasty fall and ravished her, again. After his mother's interruption and calming Beverly's concerns he'd stayed in the bedroom, sitting on the couch near the window instead of the bed for fear he'd want her to join him there. But that was simply logistics. His mind was filled with Jade and not just the woman who'd driven his desire meter way past its normal rate. No, these thoughts were different. Protectiveness and possessiveness had swarmed him where she was concerned today.

He'd been close to telling her why he really left and the pain he'd endured as a result of his actions. But he really wanted to put that behind them. He wanted to focus on the here and now.

He had no idea what Jade wanted.

In fact, he didn't know much more about Jade now then he had eight years ago. That bothered him. Just as her reason for agreeing to this charade concerned him. He couldn't convince himself that Jade was reckless and irresponsible enough to gamble with money she didn't have.

For the first time in his life Linc was baffled by a woman. Since the moment she'd walked into his office he'd thought of nothing but her and Linc wasn't used to putting this much thought into a woman. But Jade wasn't any woman. He'd known that years ago and it was even clearer now.

He'd just taken a sip of his wine when he looked up to see her walking through the entryway. She wore an ivory dress, fitting over those magnificent breasts and flowing from her waist, down those long legs to her ankles. But all that paled in comparison to the look she gave him—resolved and sensual was the only way to describe it.

"Jade, dear, are you okay?"

Linc frowned as Adam rose to meet her, dropping a kiss on her forehead. He was going to get real tired of his chivalrous brother, real quick.

She smiled. "I'm fine, Adam. It was just a little fall."

Linc's frown grew as he noted the exchange. Her high cheekbones had lifted, her hazel eyes glistening as she looked at Adam. Had she ever smiled at him that way?

"Lincoln said you were taking dinner in your room? Are you sure you're up to moving around?" Beverly asked as Adam led Jade to an empty seat.

"Those pain killers the doc gave me worked wonders," she said with another smile. "I feel just fine now."

"Horses can be very dangerous creatures. You should be more careful," Trent offered with a scowl of his own.

For a minute she only stared at him. Then, because he was sitting right next to her, she reached out, placing a hand over his, and grinned. "I'll keep that in mind next time, Trent. Thanks for your concern."

And when Linc thought his forehead would remain in that crunched up-position Trent's face softened. "Maybe big brother should keep a better eye on you."

Linc's teeth clenched. Since when did his brothers, of all people, turn on him for a woman? "She said she was fine, didn't she?" he growled.

"No thanks to you," Henry murmured. "You

should have let her ride Daisy. Lily is skittish. I'm going to have the vet look at her again this week to see what we can do about that."

His whole family was against him. Linc chanced a look at her, knowing instinctively it would be a mistake. She was eating her steak and roasted potatoes, chatting amiably with Trent, of all people, and Adam. She seemed to fit right in. That should have bothered him. And a couple of months ago it probably would have. But tonight it only enforced the feelings he was still trying to figure out.

On the other hand she was a beautiful employee. Her ebony hair was loose, falling to her shoulders like a sheet of silk. Her shoulders were bare again, the thin straps of her dress lying seductively against bronzed skin. Her eyes—which he now noticed were slanted a bit upward at the ends lending her an exotic look—shimmered with pure happiness. In them, at this moment, he saw no pretenses, no signs of manipulation.

It had been his experience with women, and shared knowledge between the brothers, that they could be the most manipulative creatures on the face of the earth. Yet, he didn't get that impression with Jade. His instincts told him she was honest and trustworthy.

Linc's thoughts were interrupted when Jade

went into depth regarding her future plans. Beauty and brains were a dangerous combination.

"Have you ever been to the Spa at the Bellagio?" She was talking to Adam but didn't wait for a response. "That's my inspiration. I want a high-class place that will cater to people who don't quite have enough money to visit the Bellagio. There's a great spot just south of the Strip that I think will attract that specific clientele. Actually I figured I'm just close enough to the Strip to get some of its straggling tourists and just far enough away not to be grouped into its price range. A spa with a personal touch and staff who get to know our clients so when they return conversation is easy and genuine. Sort of like Linc's employees."

She looked directly at him and his gut clenched.

"I noticed that at the Gramercy you knew all your employees by their first name and you talked to them like they were real people and not just a name on the payroll. I like that." She smiled then sipped her wine.

This smile wasn't like the one she'd given Adam or Trent or his father, for that matter. This one was only for him. He liked that. "It's good for morale. I took a few HR classes in college because I really didn't want to be the hated kind of boss. Did you take HR or business at Harvard?"

She shook her head. "Neither. I studied and received a degree in psychology. Then I graduated and went to massage school. My grandmother just about had a heart attack."

Beverly gave a chuckle. "I don't blame her. But at least you knew what you wanted to do. Lincoln was that way. He always knew he'd be his own boss. He never even considered going to work for the family."

"Yeah, Linc's his own man, that's for sure," Adam said snidely.

Linc, who was sitting beside him, kicked him beneath the table. "I was simply goal-oriented. And I still am." Only now his goal was becoming more personal, he thought as he gazed at Jade.

"Really?" Tilting her head in question Jade stared at him. "Now that you own the casino what do you want to do? Buy the Strip?"

Adam openly laughed. "That sounds just like Linc."

Trent and Mr. Donovan readily agreed.

Linc paused, her question having touched on a subject he'd been giving lots of thought lately. "I have some ideas in the works." Ideas he didn't think she was ready to hear.

"I'm sure you have it all planned out," Jade said confidently then launched into a conversation with Trent about law enforcement.

Linc continued to watch her, to listen to her, to really get a look at the woman he'd hired to be his date.

Jade needed to make a call. The equipment she'd ordered yesterday should have arrived at the shop today. Noelle hadn't called her to confirm delivery even though she'd left her a message to do so.

For a split second—about as long as it took for Linc to stand to the side and with a flourish of his arm signal for her to enter the room ahead of him—she felt a stab of guilt.

He'd told her to go shopping. Hell, he'd even handed her the credit card. Now any living, breathing man with the brains she knew Linc had, knew that was mistake number one in the financial handbook.

As she strolled into the room running her fingers through her hair then reaching for the lace of her sandal, she remembered that he had instructed her to purchase clothes for this week. Any idiot could conclude that to mean clothes and not equipment for the spa, yet she'd purposefully glossed over that bit of common sense and made the purchases.

She told herself he owed her, that this was fitting to what he'd put her through. That was her defense and she was sticking to it.

He came up behind her putting a hand over hers. "Don't take them off just yet," he said in a seductive voice.

Her body trembled as she let him take her hand and stood straight in front of him. He towered above her, his masculine aura surrounding her in a shield of protection. He looked down at her and for one moment in time she felt like she was the only woman in his world. His eyes drank of her, greedily taking in all that he possibly could and she withered in his embrace. "Linc, this…this thing between us—" she began.

He dropped a featherlight kiss on her forehead. "Is pretty damn powerful," he finished.

That was an understatement, she thought as she inhaled the heady scent that was all male, all female torture. Her hands came to his chest and she battled for control. Each time he touched her the fact that this was a job, that she'd just come out of a disastrous relationship, that there was no way a man like Linc could be with a woman like her, slipped from her mind. But she had to remain in control. That was the only way she'd survive. And she definitely planned to survive Lincoln Donovan this time.

"Get undressed," she stated simply before she chickened out.

His cheek was aligned with hers as he was in

the process of kissing her earlobe when she'd made her command. He paused, slanted her a curious glance. "Excuse me?"

Oh, he was a smug one, she thought wryly. He could order her around but she wasn't allowed to do the same. Well, they'd just see about that. Standing on tiptoe she nipped his chin, then took his bottom lip between her teeth, tugged and watched as his eyes darkened. Releasing him she stroked her tongue over the spot in consolation and moved forward attempting to take the kiss deeper...to take control. She pulled back shaking her head negatively. "I stripped for you. Now I want you to strip for me."

She backed out of his grasp and smiled as he continued to stare at her. "I can do that," he said confidently.

With a motion of her arms she moved farther away from him to flick on a lamp. "Then go ahead, Mr. Donovan. The floor is yours."

He backed away with a grin appearing on his face as his hands fell first to his belt. He undid it and went directly to the snap of his pants then pulled down the zipper.

"Wait a minute." Jade held up her hands. "Take your time, I want to savor this moment."

"You're enjoying this aren't you?"

She licked her lips. "Immensely."

Linc slipped off his shoes then turned his back to her. Pushing his pants slowly over his hips he bent over to step out of each pant leg. Jade ran a finger over her lip, mesmerized by the sight in front of her. He was a boxers man and he had a great ass!

Full of himself and proudly erect Linc turned to face her again. His fingers went to the rim of his shirt and he pulled it over his head. That chest that she'd felt more times today than the law allowed was bared before her. Thick pectorals, abs that would put a six-pack to shame and those powerful arms that she remembered holding her legs in the air, were bare and tantalizing. She shifted in the chair as her center throbbed insistently.

"Are you okay?" he asked with a lifted brow.

She licked her lips nervously, not a hundred percent sure how long her control would last. "I'm just fine." And so are you, she thought. "Keep it moving."

He could have tortured her. He could have taken a painfully long time to rid himself of his boxers but instead he pushed them down quickly and in two long strides stood directly in front of her, hands on his hips and at perfect attention.

Jade sucked in a breath as his male pride stood only inches away from her face. Her mouth watered and she longed to lean forward, to take him in one long, deep gulp. But something told her that's just what the almighty Lincoln expected. So gathering her wits she looked up at him and smiled. "Very nice. Now lie on the bed."

That smug grin slipped and he stared at her in question. "Jade?"

She stood, her body sliding sinuously against his as she did. "On the bed, Linc. It's right over there," she whispered. He didn't move so she gave him a little push. "Don't dawdle."

Over his shoulder he tossed her a heated look. "Is this little game almost over?" he practically growled.

She giggled. He was more than agitated, she thought with glee. She was proud of herself. In just a few short minutes she was going to make the mighty Lincoln fall. "Nope. Climb onto the bed, big boy. Facedown."

He grumbled something but she wasn't trying to hear it, she was so enthralled in his long mocha limbs stretching out before her like a journey of muscles and planes that she couldn't wait to experience. So without further ado she straddled that gorgeous rear end, giving it a teasing smack just before lifting her dress higher and settling her now moist center onto him.

"I wonder if in all this time you've spent

working, you've ever taken the time to have a massage."

"Jade, now is not the time for a damned massage," he grumbled, his voice muffled by the pillow beneath him.

She put her hands flat on his back, ran them over the taut skin until she came to his shoulders then squeezed. "Oh, sweetie, now is the perfect time. You're quite tense, Lincoln."

He swore. She worked the muscles in his shoulders until they sobbed and relaxed beneath her ministrations. Then, because she couldn't resist, she dropped a kiss in the center of his back. "You really shouldn't neglect yourself this way. You have the means to cater to your body so it's an awful shame that you don't."

"I know just what my body needs." Beneath her he rolled his hips and she moved up and down above him.

She smiled then licked the spot she'd just kissed. "I'm sure you do. But tonight I'm going to give you something extra." With her tongue she made lazy circles up and down his torso rubbing his muscles as she did. He tasted mildly salty and ever so tantalizing. Her nipples stretched against the material of her dress and she thought she'd die if he didn't touch them. But this wasn't his show so she'd have to make do as best she

could. Shrugging out of the straps she bared her
breasts then leaned over him so that her nipples
brushed against his skin.

Linc sucked in a breath then reached behind
himself to grab for her. She playfully dodged his
touch. "Not yet."

Her hands went to work and she massaged him
some more, this time going from his shoulders to
his feet and back up again. She used the relaxing
Swedish massage method, with long, even strokes
that would improve his circulation and release all
his muscle tension. She spent a lot of time on that
scrumptious backside, soliciting lewd remarks
from him in the process. She worked him for more
than a half hour, with the thought of being completely thorough. In actuality she couldn't get
enough of touching him. Right here, in this room,
with just the two of them she had unlimited access
to the man who had haunted her for years. And for
the first time in weeks her disdain for the male
species dissipated.

Jade wasn't quite sure when her emotions
shifted from the therapist to the woman sitting on
top of a gorgeous man but her thoughts quickly
moved to more mutual forms of pleasure. But she
didn't want to get ahead of herself. Their close call
earlier today had her thinking seriously about
whether or not sex with Linc was a smart move.

She returned to the head of the bed and bent down to check him. She was met with a low rumble and smiled victoriously. The ability to massage a person into deep slumber was one of the tricks of the trade and she'd used it to her advantage.

With steps as light as she could manage Jade left the room and went downstairs to the den. The house was pretty deserted at this time of night. That's exactly what she'd counted on.

"Hello?"

"Noelle?" Jade whispered.

"Jade?"

"Yes. It's me."

"Why are you whispering?"

"Don't worry about it. Did the equipment arrive?"

"Yeah. Where did you get money to buy it? Kent said he thought you were waiting until the first of the year to order it."

Again, guilt prickled Jade's conscience. "I had a windfall," she said flippantly.

"That's probably not all you've had since you're back with Linc."

Jade sat in the same chair Linc had occupied earlier today. She sat back tilting her head to stare up at the ceiling. "I'm not back with Linc."

Noelle sucked her teeth. "Are you staying at his house?"

"It's his parents' house."

"Is he there?"

"Yes, Noelle."

"Then you're back with him."

"It's not like that. Nothing's changed. Linc doesn't think of me like that."

"Evidently he does. You're there aren't you."

That was only logistics, Jade thought sadly. "I should go now. I'll try to call you back tomorrow."

"Okay. And Jade?"

"Yeah?"

"I know you're only there because of me and my stupidity."

"Noelle, you are not stupid. Lazy, maybe. But not stupid."

"Whatever. You wouldn't be there if it wasn't for me. So I at least want you to have some fun this week. Since Grammy died you've been going nonstop taking care of your business and me. For once in your life I want you to just think of yourself. To do something just for Jade."

Jade was about to say something sentimental and loving to her sister when she heard a sound outside the door. "Okay, Noelle, I have to go."

"Do what I said, Jay."

"Yeah. Yeah. 'Bye."

She hung up the phone then flicked the lamp on the desk off quickly. She was kneeling on the floor behind the desk when the door opened. For what seemed like forever but was probably only a few minutes she held her breath praying she wouldn't be caught. Then the door closed and she breathed a sigh of relief.

Chapter 6

It was only Tuesday and already she was way too
comfortable in this house, with these people, Jade
mused. She'd shared breakfast with the Donovans
again. That seemed to be the morning ritual.
However, this time they were joined by Mr.
Donavan's brother, Everett, who could have been
his brother's twin, his wife, Alma, and their two
boys, Maxwell and Benjamin.

More Donovan men, that's just what she
needed to jump-start her morning. After that tes-
tosterone induced gathering she simply wanted a
moment alone. There were things going through

her mind that she needed to clear in order to proceed with this job she'd gotten herself into.

She'd been so sure she could keep her feelings at bay, so positive that she could focus on the payoff at the end and not succumb to the whimsical thinking of a young girl. Now she wasn't quite sure she could pull it off. After speaking to Noelle, Jade and Linc had shared a bed last night and while nothing physical had occurred—save for the cuddling and soft murmurs of contentment—she'd awakened this morning feeling worse than ever.

His family thought they were lovers, undoubtedly in a more committed relationship than Linc had ever experienced in his life for the mere fact that he'd brought her here. But that couldn't be further from the truth. He was her employer, she his rent-a-date for the week. There were no real feelings between them, nothing that would turn into a fabulous love affair, to her belief. And the fact that she was technically still recovering from a botched affair coupled with her guilt over this new deception—Jade was weighed down with a supreme sense of loss.

With a sigh she stood from the chair on which she'd been lounging. There was a cookout for lunch and a dinner party tonight. She estimated she had about two and a half hours to herself before she was on duty again and had decided to spend that time swimming. So as not to waste another minute she slipped out of her robe and walked to the edge of the pool. Sparkling water tempted her and she stuck a toe in first to test the temperature then with a giggle dove in.

Each lap was invigorating, restoring the energy she felt slowly slipping from her as she worked to keep up this pretense. It was a means to an end, she kept telling herself. If not for Charles and his underhanded scheme she wouldn't be in this predicament at all. If not for Noelle, whom, because of her caring words last night, she couldn't even be angry with anymore. Jade tried to shake the pity off. She could almost hear Grammy saying "there's no use crying over spilled milk."

So she wouldn't dwell on what Charles did anymore. She'd allowed him to deceive her and she accepted that. She allowed Noelle to lean on her and depend on her. But it was time for a change.

He'd entered from the door farthest to the back, the one accessible from the gym. After putting himself through a vigorous workout this morning Linc had thought a few laps in the pool would help calm this raging storm building within him. A storm that centered around Jade. It was just his luck that she'd be there at that very moment.

She lay on a lounge chair and looked to be in deep thought. He'd stood quietly in the corner wondering if he should simply turn around and leave. But as it always seemed to happen when she was near, he couldn't take his eyes off her. A modest navy blue two-piece bathing suit adorned her body yet salacious thoughts trickled through his mind expeditiously. He was instantly aroused.

He'd gone to his bedroom last night with the express purpose of making love to her but she'd had other plans. Her touch soothed him, her close-ness lulling him like a baby. Never had he been in a bed with a woman—naked—and nothing happened. Well, something had happened. Some-thing that greatly contributed to today's decision.

Those frown lines were on her forehead again and he knew instinctively that he'd made the right decision. She stood, stretched, and his gut clenched as he remembered rolling over last night, pulling her closer to him, reveling in the warmth her body exuded. Sleeping and waking with her had felt right.

Breakfast had further proved his point. Jade had blended in with his aunt and uncle and cousins just as she had the rest of his family, just like she belonged there.

And it was along those lines that he been thinking all morning. He wanted Jade and while he wasn't sure for how long he knew undoubtedly that seven days and six nights was not enough.

She'd done a few laps and he'd finally decided to join her when that back door opened and in through it walked Trent. It didn't take him long to notice someone already occupied the pool and with a grim expression he confronted his brother. "She's, ah, something, huh?"

Linc's hands tightened on the ends of the towel he held around his neck. "Yeah, she's that."

"I've been meaning to ask you, what's she been doing for the last eight years?"

She had perfect form, her body cutting cleanly through the water. "I don't know. I didn't keep tabs on her." Although he'd never stopped thinking about her.

"Really? It seems to me like you've given her a lot of thought."

She was on her back now, those plump breasts surfacing as she moved throughout the pool. "What makes you say that?"

"You wouldn't have brought her here without giving it some thought. That's not who you are. And the way you're watching her... I don't know, it makes me think you're considering more than just a week's stay."

"Is there something wrong with that?" Linc asked, unable to deny that Trent's words were true.

Trent shrugged. "Only that you don't know very much about her. And why did she agree to spend the week with you after not seeing you for eight years?"

"Why is that any of your concern?"

Trent continued to watch him. "It's not. But you are. I know you're quite aware of women's habits to manipulate wealthy, successful men. I simply want you to be careful."

"She's not after my money," Linc said vehemently. That was the last thing he'd accuse Jade of.

"How do you know that for sure? You haven't seen her for eight years, then she magically appears and you invite her home for the celebration. Could be she knew about the anniversary, knew about your success with the casino and decided the time was right."

"What are you saying?" He really didn't want to know. His reunion with Jade was purely coincidental. After all, who would purposefully lose five thousand dollars in his casino just to get a chance at him? That didn't make much sense…and all of a sudden it made a lot of sense.

"I'm saying don't be fooled by the gorgeous body and the pretty smile. Think about what you're doing and find out exactly who you're doing it with." Trent sighed. "Look, I like her, too. I didn't want to but she sort of grows on you." He gave a wry grin toward the pool. "But the fact remains that you don't know diddly about this woman or her motives. So I'm telling you to watch your back."

Although Trent had definitely given him something to think about Linc wasn't about to admit it to him. Instead he laughed it off. "I thought that's what my kid brothers were for."

"Hey, that's what I'm doing here. I'm watching your back because that little lady is in the process of wrapping you around her little finger and I wanted to be sure you were aware that you were being reeled in and that you're prepared for it."

"Don't worry. I'm prepared for whatever comes my way where Jade is concerned."

The cookout had been a blast except for one minor incident. Jade remembered the afternoon soiree while she dressed for the evening.

She'd arrived on Linc's arm prepared to smile and exchange small talk with his parents, family and friends for a couple of hours. Lawn chairs were spread from the terrace to the garden entrance and then again near the outside pool. There were at least seventy-five people there, mingling and partaking of the generous food laid out for them.

They bumped into Ben and Adam first, who immediately borrowed her for the fourth in a card game. Linc hadn't seemed too crazy about the idea of her going with them, but then again Adam and Ben hadn't asked his permission.

That began an enjoyable afternoon except by that time she hadn't seen much of Linc. The few times she'd spotted him he was with a group of men looking serious as they talked. She'd seen him again, this time being approached by a pretty woman. Startled at first by the sight of Linc with another woman she quickly surmised that they did not look good together at all. That was a strange thought. It seemed petty and too much like a jealous or jilted lover. She felt possessive and longed to go over and tell the trick to get lost. That's when she remembered that Linc was not her man. She had no business trying to block another woman's shot at him.

Then again, she did. The terms of her employment stated that she was his date for the week. That gave her full possession of him—for seven days at least. Here she was in a fake relationship and already losing her man. With a spark of anger growing she moved in the direction where the traitorous male stood. She was damned tired of being the fool in this game of love. And she had absolutely no intention of letting another man get the best of her. Charles had done a good enough job of that.

She approached just as the woman threw her head back and laughed at something Linc said. Her manicured nails glittered as she ran her hands over Linc's shoulders. Except for a twitch of his jaw, Linc seemed to be quite comfortable with the exchange. Jade, however, was not.

"Hello," she said brightly.

The woman turned, her smile slipping ever so slightly. Jade extended a hand to the crooning minx. "I'm Jade Vincent. And you are?"

Reluctantly, the woman shook Jade's hand. "Leslie Kindle."

"Nice to meet you, Leslie. And it's been very nice of you to keep Lincoln company while I was away." With that she moved to stand beside Linc, ignoring the bemused expression on his face.

"Vincent? The name isn't familiar to me," Leslie said.

Jade didn't miss the woman's subtle hint. She wasn't a part of their social circle and she wasn't trying to be. But she would not be disrespected.

"It wouldn't be since I don't know you. But thank you again for keeping Linc company." Jade gave her a bright-as-white smile that secretly said "your trick didn't work so keep it moving."

Leslie Kindle didn't quite know what else to say and when Adam suddenly appeared whisking the woman away to retrieve a cool beverage Jade felt a moment of relief that was replaced again by an aura of disdain the moment Linc spoke.

"Candy-coated sarcasm. I never would have guessed you had that in you," he said with a fabulous smile.

Jade looked up at him, hating the hint of pleasure she saw on his face. "I never would have expected such blatant rudeness from you. But then you are one of the Triple Threat Donovans."

After his mention of his reputation the other day she'd made a point to find out the details. It hadn't been hard. In fact, Adam had been more than eager to fill her in. The fact that they'd lived in the same city and she'd never heard these rumors only served to prove they were from different worlds.

But for right now, for this week, they were together and dammit he was going to act like it!

His amusement slipped as he now glowered at her. "I see you do have some knowledge of my reputation."

"That doesn't bother you, does it?"

"What? The fact that you've heard the rumors?" He slipped his hands into his pockets and momentarily looked away.

That twitch in his jaw was back and for a moment she was tempted to touch him there, to smooth the tension away, but she refrained.

"I have no control over what people say."

"You have control over your actions. You asked me here to be your date. I didn't know that included being one of your harem."

"I do not have a harem," he said tightly.

Jade didn't like the way this conversation was going. It was as if she were a jealous girlfriend, when, in fact, she should have been the exact opposite. Another woman with Linc would keep him away from her. This would definitely keep her from entertaining foolish thoughts of a future with him. Ironically, that bit of knowledge didn't make her like seeing him with another woman any more. "Be that as it may, I would appreciate you holding up your end of the bargain until this week is over."

"Me? Hold up my end?" he bellowed.

Jade noticed a number of curious glances turning their way. She pasted on a fake smile when she really felt like cursing his arrogance at the top of her lungs.

"You're the one laughing it up with my cousins and my brothers."

"Well, at least they were willing to pay some attention to me," she said, trying to keep her voice low.

Exasperated and just a tiny bit pleased at the prospect that she really did want to be with him, Linc took her by the arm and led her through the crowd until they were alone at the edge of the bushes leading to the garden. He wanted to shake some sense into her, to tell her that he wanted nothing more than to get rid of all these people and shower her with his brand of special attention. She'd invaded his every thought for the past two days but for the last few hours he hadn't had a moment alone with her. Each time he'd seen her with one of his brothers or his cousins he'd wanted to yell and pull her away, but he'd refrained. But that was over now. He was going to make damn sure she knew that her place was with him.

He pulled her just beyond the garden entrance where they could no longer be seen by the guests. His hands cupped her face and he watched as shock overtook her moments before he captured her lips with his own. With an urgency he'd never experienced Linc kissed her, pouring all his jealousy, all his arousal into that one passion-filled action.

She grasped his arms, tried to hold herself aloof then succumbed.

Breathless seconds later he rested his forehead on hers trying to calm his erratic breathing. "Never doubt that you have my full attention. Always."

"I…" She took deep breaths. "I'm not used to this."

He kissed her temple, the tip of her nose then

the outline of her cheek. "You're not used to being kissed?" he whispered.

"No." She smiled, her hands relaxing on his chest. "I'm not used to this togetherness charade. Your family expects us to be a happy couple."

Linc pulled back to look at her. "Haven't you ever been part of happy couple, Jade?"

She didn't answer, but tried to look away. Touching a finger to her chin Linc turned her back to face him.

"Where's your boyfriend? Your husband?" he implored. "Tell me why a beautiful woman like you is still alone?"

She shrugged. "Apparently beauty's not such a hot commodity anymore."

"Maybe the population of foolish men is growing." He stroked her cheek wondering if that population included him.

"It doesn't matter." She moved out of his grasp to stand near a bush with huge yellow flowers.

Linc had never been an outdoorsman, but could not deny the beautiful landscape and the way it perfectly framed this alluring woman. "How did he hurt you?" he asked without crowding her.

She didn't face him. "He didn't."

"Are you sure?"

There was a pregnant pause.

"He disappointed me. He was just one in a long line of men who disappointed me."

Her words were soft yet they sliced through him like a hot blade. He was one of those men, he knew without asking. Eight years ago he'd left her in that room and hadn't returned.

"I'm sorry," he said for lack of any other words.

She turned to him then. "Don't be. It's my fault. I made myself vulnerable. It's only right that I accept the consequences of my actions."

Was carrying around a disdainful attitude toward all men a consequence? Was holding herself at arm's length her fate in life to keep from being let down again? Linc couldn't bring himself to accept that. She deserved so much more.

But could he give it to her?

He moved to her side, slowly took her hand and brought her fingers to his lips. "Don't blame yourself for the stupidity of others. If they disappointed you, then they weren't worth your time."

She stared up at him quizzically.

"That includes the younger, immature Lincoln Donovan."

She smiled then and Linc felt a grip on his heart he was sure should have caused some type of pain. Instead it invigorated him. It confirmed that being with her was right.

"Thank you," she whispered.

He nodded but realized he didn't want her gratitude. What he wanted from Jade Vincent he wasn't so sure she was willing to give.

Jade had the suite to herself as she showered and now slipped into her evening gown.

Fastening diamond earrings to her lobes she reminded herself again that Linc was simply her employer. That she had no right to be angry with him for spending time with those other women this afternoon. However, her little display of jealousy had ended quite pleasingly. Never would she have guessed that such simple words could mean so much. But when they'd come from Linc they'd meant more than she could explain.

"It's just business. Just business," she repeated until the knock at the door stopped her. "Come in," she bellowed.

The door opened and in a swish of lavender chiffon Beverly entered. "Good. You're dressed. Lincoln is busy so I've come to take you downstairs."

Jade turned to face her. "You look great," she said honestly.

Beverly smiled, did a little turn in the middle of the floor then went to Jade, taking one of her hands. "Thank you, dear. You look wonderful, too. Your complexion is perfect for jewel tones."

Jade looked down at her sapphire-blue dress and reluctantly agreed. This was one of her new dresses. One the clerk in Saks had picked out for her. She wasn't overly fond of the plunging neckline and non-existent back, but she had to admit it made her feel sexy. And if you just looked at her you'd think she really belonged in this house with these people.

"Lincoln is going to love it," Beverly said.

Her heart fluttered at the thought. "Do you really think so?"

"Child, please. I know my son and if there's one thing he loves as much as business, it's a beautiful woman."

"I'm sure he does love beautiful women, of his own class," Jade murmured and continued to stare down at her dress, rubbing her free hand down the front of the dress.

"Pardon me?" Beverly moved a step closer.

Had she said that aloud? Jade looked up into the older woman's face and stammered, "Ah, I just meant that I'm, ah, sure Lincoln loves all beautiful women."

Beverly looked at her questioningly and Jade prayed she hadn't just screwed up the charade she was hired to portray. She hadn't meant to verbalize her apprehension about being the kind of woman Linc liked. That was a point of doubt she'd kept strictly to herself all these years.

Beverly reached out and touched Jade's chin, lifting her head up. "Lincoln is really taken with you, with or without this dress."

"You think so?" Why did her voice suddenly sound so needy? Jade wondered.

Beverly studied her another moment. "Is there something wrong, Jade? Something between you and Lincoln?"

Jade turned away and changed the subject. She wanted so badly to confide in someone, to tell just how confused she was on the inside. On the other hand she knew that the only reason she was here with Linc was because she owed him money and he viewed this as a way to be repaid. She hadn't dared entertain the thought that she was still in love with Linc. And wasn't fool enough to believe it was impossible.

In the span of a few days she'd turned into a liar and a thief. The fact that Beverly stood in front of her speaking about a fake relationship made this even worse. She liked Beverly. If truth be told she liked all the Donovans. And she felt like a colossal jerk for betraying them this way. But what other choice did she have? There was so much more at stake here than her feelings.

So as the two women made their way down the stairs and into the main ballroom Jade squared her shoulders and swore she'd get it together. She had four more days to go. She could do this. She had to do this. Next week, when she was in the comfort of her own home, her own world, she'd allow herself a day or two of sadness.

His tie was too tight.

That's the reason Linc gave for being agitated the moment he walked into the room. A majority of the guests had already arrived. He blamed that on the conference call he was forced to take an hour before the party began.

His mother would most certainly have his head, but decorum would warrant she wait until *after* the meal.

Oddly enough, she wasn't the woman who pre-occupied his thoughts. They'd returned to the cookout, hand in hand. What just last week had been an enigma to him was slowly revealing itself. For the first time in his life Linc admitted that he wanted something more in his life. Jade was that something.

She'd been hurt and apparently it was so bad that she was determined not to make the same mistake twice. He could understand that and viewed gaining her trust as a high priority. At the same time he also acknowledged that clearing a five-thousand-dollar debt was a big deal to her. He had lots of questions as to why, so he'd finally given in and done a preliminary background check on her. He could have just asked but was fairly certain she wasn't willing to tell him.

The brief background check had shown that not only was she a licensed masseuse but she owned her own spa, right off the Strip as she'd said last night at dinner. He wondered why she'd neglected to mention that fact. Moreover, he wondered why, if she owned her own business, she'd gambled away five thousand dollars and couldn't afford to pay it back.

He'd be lying if he said that Trent's words hadn't planted a certain amount of doubt in his mind but he wasn't yet ready to believe that Jade's goal was as unscrupulous as Trent thought. While he didn't know the facts of her life Linc was sure of a few things where Jade was concerned. For example, he was certain that the look on Jade's face when he'd taken her riding, the sound of her voice as she'd called his name when they'd gotten caught up in the bathroom, the touch of her hands as she'd massaged him, were not fake. No actress could be that good.

She wasn't manipulating him for money. If anything he was probably the one doing the manipulating. With other debts he'd taken collateral and in some rare instances promissory notes. But from Jade he'd wanted more. And he'd gotten it so far. But it still wasn't enough.

That fact was the root of his disgruntled mood this evening. He wanted Jade and he wanted to tell her this as soon as possible. He wanted to tell her that his reasons for asking her here went far beyond the debt. But he hadn't had a moment alone with her today to do that.

With deliberate steps he made his way through the crowd stopping to shake hands with men he hadn't seen in a while and kiss the cheeks of women he wished he hadn't seen in a while. Despite his mother's warning there weren't as many eligible women here as he'd first expected. A couple of daughters from the socialite circle but not nearly as many as he'd anticipated. Then again, the presence of Leslie Kindle was enough. Momentarily he thought back to this afternoon when Jade had interrupted them. He'd been touched by her jealousy and proud of the way she'd handled Leslie. He certainly planned to avoid the woman for the duration of the week's celebrations.

In the distance the band began to play. The crowd seemed to dissipate with most of the guests heading toward their tables and a few going straight to the dance floor. He hated to dance and decided to hang back a bit and scan the tables until he found Jade. Slipping his hands in his pockets he took position near a lighted ficus, hopefully out of easy view of the socialite mistresses. His attention was piqued at the sound of sultry laughter and he turned to the direction from whence it had come. His body came alive with desire as his gaze found her.

There she was, wearing a dress—a dress that showed way too much of her gorgeous skin—head thrown back, laughing at something Max had said as he glided over the dance floor with her. It was an upbeat song yet he didn't miss Max's hands around her waist. He clenched his teeth and was about to step onto the dance floor and forego his distaste of dancing when he felt a hand on his elbow.

"She's a gem, Lincoln. I'm so glad you two reunited."

Linc frowned. He thought for sure his mother would wait to approach him until later. Apparently he'd been wrong. He really wasn't in the mood to discuss his tardiness right now. "Great party, Mother," he said stiffly.

Beverly looked around the room. "It's a good kick off. Just wait until the rest of the week unfolds," she said contentedly.

"Where's your happy husband?"

She chuckled. "He's just like his son, taking care of some last-minute business over there with a couple of stable owners from across town. But I'm more concerned with why you aren't with Jade?"

"I was going to claim her when you stopped me."

"Oh, well, then that was a good move on my part. Son, you look a little disturbed. I can only assume it's a touch of the green-eyed monster and I wanted to let you know that there's no need for it."

Green-eyed monster? What was she talking about now? "Mother, I assure you, you have no idea what's going through my mind right now."

"Humph. I'm not as old as you think I am and I'm certainly no fool. I know when a man is jealous. And while I think it's cute, Jade might not feel that way."

His teeth clenched as Ben walked onto the dance floor and interrupted the rendezvous between Max and Jade. Then his mother's words registered and he glanced at her. "I'm not normally the jealous type," he stated slowly.

Beverly made a big production of wiping non-existent lint from his shoulders and straightening his tie. "And she's no normal woman." With a hand to his cheek she smiled up at him. "There's only one way to combat jealousy." She paused and when he didn't respond continued, "Pay attention to your woman or another man will."

That's the same thing Jade had told him. "She's—" He opened his mouth to speak but was quieted by her hand hovering inches from his lips.

"She's a beautiful woman with a lot of spirit and a zest for life that you seem to have forgotten. However, she's with you for a reason. Stop being too stubborn to see it."

With a smooth movement he grasped his mother's wrist, brought the back of her hand to his lips and kissed it. "I know full well the reason she's with me."

Beverly blushed at the devilish twinkle in her son's eye and pulled her hand away. "Then act like it."

With that tidbit of advice she left him alone. Jade was still on the dance floor, still having a good time without him and he frowned. He was just about to go out and retrieve her when again he was detained.

"Enjoying the party, Lincoln?" his cousin, Max, asked.

"I would be if people would stop interrupting me."

"My bad." Max chuckled. "That's quite a woman

you've got there." He nodded toward the dance floor, toward Jade.

"I would say I'm glad you've noticed but I'm not."

Max's smile broadened. "Possessive, huh? Trent said he thought you were slipping."

"What? Because I don't want to share my date, I'm slipping." Linc didn't know why he was even entertaining this conversation. One thing the Donovan men did well was goad each other. They were a competitive bunch. But in the end their loyalty to each other would prevail. They had each other's back, that was for sure.

Laughing Max clapped a hand on Linc's shoulder. "I'm not saying you don't have a right to be possessive. She's quite a woman, like I said. I'm about to place my bet on how long it'll be before you fall."

Linc didn't like Max's implication, no matter how close to the truth it was. What he had in mind for Jade was between them. His family had nothing to do with it and he wasn't in the mood for their unsolicited advice.

"That's a fool's bet," Linc said as he watched Adam and Jade walk through the terrace doors. His body tensed but he didn't say a word.

Max had watched their departure as well and his smile broadened. "I doubt that," he was saying but Linc didn't hear him because he was already making long strides across the room.

Earlier Jade had made a point of reprimanding him about keeping up the pretense of the relationship. Now it seemed he was going to have to remind her of the same thing. For a woman with a grudge against men she certainly kept their company well. He took a deep breath and tried to calm himself. All he wanted was the chance to be alone with her, to tell her all these things he'd been feeling and how she was affecting him, changing the way he thought about his future.

Jade was smiling on the outside yet anything but happy on the inside. She hadn't seen Linc at all this evening and had long since admitted that she missed him. Their time in the garden had put him in a new light in her eyes. The way he'd looked at her like she was the most important person in the world. His touch had been gentle and, she thought, sincere. She desperately wanted him to touch her like that again. She knew that these feelings were dangerous but was helpless against their flourishing.

Adam thought she needed some air so he'd offered a walk outside near the pool. Air wasn't what she needed but she was too polite to turn him down. So now she was walking beneath the stars with one man while thoughts of his brother ran rampant through her mind. Then, as if conjured from her thoughts, he appeared. She heard his voice from behind but had already felt his presence.

"Jade?"

His voice seemed calm but when she turned to look at him the first thing she noticed was his stormy eyes. "Lincoln," she whispered.

"Well, it's about time you arrived," Adam said. "With a date as fine as Jade you'd think you would be on time."

Although Adam laughed Linc apparently didn't find anything funny. He kept his eyes trained on Jade.

"I…wasn't sure what time you'd finally get here," she said, butterflies dancing merrily in the pit of her stomach.

"I'm here now."

She'd already released Adam's hand and now twiddled with the beads on her handbag. "Yes. You are."

Linc took a step toward her. "Come here."

She took a step closer to him and saw that his entire body was tense. He looked angry but she wasn't quite sure. Then she realized that Adam was still standing there. "Adam was just keeping me company."

Linc spared Adam a glance. "He doesn't have to do that anymore."

Adam grinned. "Yeah, I can see I've been dumped," he said with a look to Jade.

"I'm sorry," she whispered.

"No. Don't apologize. You're right where you belong," Adam said and looked at Linc.

Linc didn't want to think about the grief he was going to get from his brother when he was alone. In fact, he didn't care. All he cared about right now was being with her. She looked spectacular and the urge to touch her was becoming unbearable. He reached out to take her arm.

"We should be getting back inside," she said.

Linc watched as Adam retreated, moving his hand up and down her arm. They were finally alone and he didn't want to chance that changing. "We're not going back to the party."

"We're not?"

He shook his head negatively and pulled her against him. This was where he liked her most, in his arms, looking up at him as if he were the only man in her life. Linc readily acknowledged that he liked the sound of that.

"I want to be alone with you." His hands stroked her back, loving the feel of her warm curves against him.

"Oh?" she said then looked away.

He pulled back and stared down at her. "Does that surprise you?"

She shrugged then faced him again. "A little."

"Why?"

"Because our agreement was to put on a show for your family. When we're alone there's no reason for the show. I mean, I know I'm not the type of woman you're usually with so it surprises me that you'd willingly want to be alone with me. Again."

Linc wasn't sure but he didn't think he was going to like the implications of what she was saying. "You're going to have to explain that to me, Jade. We've been alone together before and in my opinion have both enjoyed ourselves immensely. You do remember the massage last night, the bath yesterday?"

Jade stared at him. "Of course I remember. It's just..." She didn't know how to say it. Didn't know why she'd even brought it up. She thought she'd resigned herself to the facts and decided to proceed from there. Apparently her brain had a different agenda.

"It's just what?" he prodded. "Don't be afraid to talk to me, Jade. I want to hear what you have to say."

There it was again, that soft caress of his voice over her skin, that shiver of excitement she got when she had his undivided attention. She didn't know how to react. What she did know was that it was time to lay her cards on the table. She was attracted to Linc, there was no doubt about that. And he was physically attracted to her, that was also clear. Beyond that…

"We're from different worlds, Linc. I'm sure that fact hasn't skipped your mind."

"Actually, I thought we were two people living in Las Vegas. But if you want to tell me you're from another planet or something, go right ahead and enlighten me." He gave her a wry smile.

She wasn't amused. "Don't play. You know what I mean. I'm not a part of your social class. You know it and you knew it before." She pulled out of his grasp then and turned away because looking at him while he acknowledged there was no future for them was too painful to bear. "That's why you left," she said quietly.

Linc thrust his hands into his pockets but did not move to follow her. "Is that what you thought? That I left you because you didn't have the same advantages that I did?"

"It was obvious."

"Really? Then obviously Harvard has lowered its standard on accepting the smartest students with the most potential."

She turned and glared at him.

"That's the stupidest thing I've ever heard, Jade. If you really thought that low of me then why did you sleep with me? Why did you even give me the time of day?"

"I…" She opened her mouth to speak but the words were lost. She shook her head instead and took a deep breath. "I liked you."

"And I liked you." He closed the distance between them. "I knew who and what you were and I still liked you. I liked you enough to ask you to my room. I liked you enough to make slow, sweet love to you because I knew that's what you needed."

"But you didn't like me enough to stay."

Her words sliced through him and he reached out to touch her then. He cupped her face, leaned forward and kissed her forehead and was profoundly grateful that she didn't pull away. He didn't know if he could handle her pulling away from him right now. He was about to be more honest than he ever had with any woman in his life and he needed her to at least be receptive to hearing him out. When she reached up and clasped his wrists, staring at him with all the hurt and confusion from their past, his heart weakened more.

"I liked you so much it frightened me. And that had nothing to do with social status. I knew you were a long-term type of girl. But I also knew I couldn't do long-term. I was afraid to do long-term. So I left. I convinced myself that I was doing the right thing. That we both had futures to pursue and we shouldn't be held to any type of commitment. I was wrong," he whispered. "I was so wrong and I'm sorry." He kissed the tip of her nose, then lightly brushed her lips. "Please, forgive me."

What could she say? What could she do when his words had taken all the air from her lungs? She looked up at him through tear-filled eyes and felt her heart hammering wildly in her chest.

"Linc." His name was a whisper on her lips as she searched for words.

His answer was to scoop her up into his arms.

Jade opened her mouth to protest but was quickly silenced by the crush of his lips on hers. His tongue demanded entrance as he set in motion a brutally erotic kiss that warmed every nuance of her body, her soul.

She knew what would happen next. Just as she'd known that it was inevitable. Linc was not taking her back to the party. They were headed toward his room, toward the moment Jade had secretly longed for.

Linc kicked the door closed then moved to the bed where he laid her down gently, as if she would break if he did otherwise. For endless moments they simply stared at each other, eight years of apologies and misunderstandings between them. Then his lips captured hers again.

His hands moved all over her body in soft, languid strokes that increased the heat rising at her center.

"I can't stop touching you," he whispered.

She acknowledged that fact and touched him in response. Moving her hands up and down his muscled back, tilting her head to better receive his kiss. This was what she'd dreamed of for so long.

"Can't stop wanting you," he breathed into her ear then licked her lobe.

"I wanted you, too. All these years I've wanted you." And loved you. She wisely kept that thought to herself. This moment was special, fragile. And while she wasn't a girl anymore, she didn't entertain any fantasies about what they were doing, she wasn't going to let this opportunity slip by. She deserved this one night. She deserved this one moment of happiness. And if it was all that she would ever get from Lincoln Donovan, then she was damn sure going to enjoy every minute of it.

Her tongue slid along his then moved to his lips, suckling each one into her mouth. Her fingers gripped the back of his head, holding him still while she had her way with his mouth. He groaned and she smiled.

"You're killing me."

She spread her legs and he dutifully sank between them. She thrust her center up against his rigid erection. "You ain't seen nothing yet."

"I told you what all that squirming does to me." He dipped his head, kissed the spot on her neck just beneath her ear then moved lower until his teeth sank into the skin of her shoulder. He wanted her beyond reason and that desire edged him to take her quickly, to devour her and satiate his own need.

But he remembered her words, remembered the pain he'd seen in her eyes, the pain he'd caused by the foolish actions of an immature boy. He tapped down his desire, focused on her and how much he wanted her forgiveness, her respect.

Jade moaned and gripped his shoulders. "Lincoln."

He pressed into her center again and felt her shiver beneath him, her hands gripping his shirt and twisting. He liked feeling like he was driving her as crazy as she drove him. That's another reason he planned to draw this sweet torture out for as long as possible.

That sinfully delectable dress slipped easily from her shoulders and he kissed the creamy skin of her neck down to her collarbone, finally stopping at one puckered nipple.

Grasping both breasts in his hands Linc gorged

himself, suckling and nipping until his erection pressed painfully against his zipper.

Her hands stroked his head while soft whispers of delight escaped her mouth. The sound soared through him at a rapid pace and he shook with desire. "Why are you here?" he asked in a muffled voice before licking the puckered left nipple again.

She heaved and arched against him, giving him full, unadulterated access. "I came here to be with you," she said breathily.

Linc's heart filled at her admission. His idea of keeping her longer than a week firmly cemented in his mind. No way was he giving up something this special, this intense.

"I don't like seeing you with other men," he admitted as he left a trail of heated kisses down her torso.

"I don't like seeing you with other women," she whispered.

He pulled her dress down past her hips and off her legs. She wore another bikini and he wasted no time ridding her of it along with her shoes. She was naked and beautiful. "I can't think of another woman. I'm so captivated by you."

He covered her again then dragged his lips over hers, his tongue snaking out to leave a heated trail along her mouth. She gasped and he dipped inside letting the warmth of her engulf him. For endless moments he kissed her, trying to explain what he was feeling in that one fevered motion. She didn't move, only participated in the kiss. Then her arms came around his neck and he stroked his tongue against hers with slower, more deliberate licks.

He was more than captivated. Her arms held him captive, physically. While her actions held a tight rein on his emotions.

Chapter 7

There were no slow songs playing in the background. No candles and no preamble. Each touch of his hand meant one thing and she understood him implicitly. Pulling him closer Jade sank into the kiss, welcoming each stroke and moan as if it were air. His hands were on her hips now, sliding up her sides until he brushed her breasts.

"Linc," she whispered by way of consent.

Suckling on her bottom lip he answered her plea and reached for her breasts, palming them each in his hands, toying with their hardened crests.

Her head lulled back against the pillows and his tongue traced a hot path down her throat until she quivered beneath him. Grasping each breast firmly he pushed them up until they cradled his face and then groaned his pleasure. Forcing himself to slow down he lifted his head slightly, needing to see her, to know her every reaction to his touch.

She still held his head and when he found her face, her eyes were only half opened, her tongue snaking out to slide over her lower lip. His groin tightened and he moved his hands seductively over her hips. "You're beautiful," he moaned. To emphasize his point he kissed her all over, his temperature rising steadily. How was he ever going to go slow with her? He swore and closed his eyes, resting his forehead against her stomach. "What are you doing to me?"

Without waiting for an answer he kissed along her thighs until they shook beneath him, then lifting one leg and planting it firmly on his shoulder he set out to taste her in the one way he hadn't all those years ago. From the moment he'd seen her again he'd known that this was something he couldn't let her walk out of his life again without experiencing. He quivered as he inhaled her intoxicating scent then moaned as his tongue came out to stroke her moistened folds.

Surely he had died and gone to heaven. That's exactly what she tasted like, all that was sweet and pure and tantalizingly blissful. He needed her so badly. Her leg tightened around his back, thrusting his face deeper between her legs, and he continued to devour her. He'd skipped dinner tonight but this would certainly satisfy his appetite.

Jade was in another world, her desire for Linc surpassing anything she'd ever thought to be true. In his eyes she'd seen something that he was usually careful about revealing. Linc was vulnerable. To women, to relationships, to the world, and her heart ached for him. For whatever reason he'd convinced himself that he couldn't love unconditionally and couldn't be loved the same in return. It was ridiculous, a coward's way out that she admitted to being shocked that he would take.

So tonight, if only for this one night in his life she would give him everything, all that she had would be his. Even the love that she'd kept inside for all these years. His hot mouth scorched her center and developed a rhythm, one that she freely picked up and ministered to. Inside her a storm built from small flickers of desire to lightning-quick flashes that threatened to singe her skin.

Her breasts were swollen and hot and while he was otherwise occupied she cupped them in her own hands. From his scorching kisses she'd known that Linc had a very skillful mouth but right now, as he mastered her center, pulling every drop of desire from her core, she thought what an understatement that had been. Sinuously, wickedly, she ground her center against him again and whimpered with delight.

As they said in a hurricane, she was in the eye of the storm, twisting and turning against the ravaging winds he elicited. When his tongue entered her it was the end. She screamed his name as her essence poured from her in a steady tide.

He'd stared down at her, propped up on his elbow. When her body had stopped quivering she'd searched for him, alarmed by the thought that he may have left her. Again.

"I'm right here," he said, tracing a finger along her swollen bottom lip.

She took a steadying breath and smiled up at him. "Yes, you are. But you're way overdressed."

He chuckled as she pushed his jacket over his shoulders. He finished the job for her while her fingers hastily undid the buttons on his shirt. Pushing the material quickly she couldn't wait to taste him. Her lips grazed over one tight pectoral, then took the pert nipple into her mouth. He sucked in a breath and she put her hands on him, massaging the rigid contours of his chest, his abs.

Linc ripped the shirt from his arms, groaning as

she kissed him. Her tongue stroked his navel as she unbuttoned his pants and pushed them and his boxers over his thighs. He lifted and reclined as she undressed him.

When they were both naked he pushed her back onto the bed then propped up on his elbows and stared down at her. "You are beautiful," he said as he brushed errant strands of hair from her face. "I don't remember you being this beautiful before."

"Make love to me, Lincoln. Not like you did back then, but like you want to now."

His entire body rocked with emotion. Had she read his mind? He'd just been thinking that this would be like their first time because now he saw her in an entirely new light. He saw them in a new light. She wanted him still and he wanted her, more than he'd ever wanted another woman before or since.

So with slow, deliberate movements he leaned in closer to take her lips. He took his time savoring her mouth, building the passion between them until it emanated from her every pore. She squirmed beneath him and ran her hands over him communicating her need, her yearning for him. He continued to kiss her all over, to drink in her responsiveness and claim it for his own. He kissed her breasts, loving the feel of the plump globes between his lips most. The he kissed her stomach, her thighs. The backs of her thighs, her fingers, her palms. He wanted every part of her, every nuance to be touched by him and never forgotten by her.

His arousal lengthened and stiffened, and burned for her. He wanted to go slow, to draw this mating dance out for as long as he could but knew that he'd never make it. Then she whispered, "Now." And he was saved.

He reached toward the nightstand and retrieved a box of condoms. Quickly retrieving one foil packet he ripped it open and sheathed himself. With one hand he spread her thighs wider then stroked her already damp folds and moaned. "Yes. Now."

And without another word he slipped inside her. In one long, torturously slow movement filling her completely. For endless moments they stayed perfectly still, joined as one.

When he began to move, taking deep, soul-shattering thrusts Jade lifted her legs and wrapped them around his waist. Her hands held him close by the back and she closed her eyes as his thick erection moved in and out of her. She was slick and he was hard. She was open and accommodating and he was demanding, yet sensual. They were perfect together, just like he remembered.

He was whispering in her ear, saying things he hadn't known existed in his mind. She was holding him so tightly, both with her arms and within her sweet walls. With each dive in and reluctant pull out Linc felt something slipping from inside of him, something he'd been holding on to for far too long. She kissed his ear, her tongue lathing his lobe and beneath. She told him how good he was, how good he felt and while he'd heard all this before, coming from her it made him feel like he was on top of the world. He realized then that her opinion of him mattered. Whether it was of him as a lover or of him as a man, it simply mattered.

She rocked her hips to meet him until he thought he'd go crazy with lust. Placing his hands on her hips he held her still and plundered into her with the rising fury of a volcano about to erupt.

"I missed you," he said with each fierce movement. Then he paused as if his words had shocked even him. "From the moment I left you eight years ago until the second you walked into my office I've missed you." He stared down at her and wanted to hear her response, to see her reaction.

Her eyes fluttered open even as he slammed his length into her again. Her head thrashed on the pillows as she felt that magnificent wave of pleasure threatening to take her again. "Linc," she said breathlessly. "Don't." She couldn't take the intrusion. This time was special. It was a homecoming of sorts, a cherished moment that she didn't want blemished. He whispered the words again in her ear and she felt the tears begin to fall.

Lifting a hand he kneaded her breasts then toyed with her nipple until she moaned. "How does it feel, Jade?"

She moaned.

"How do I make you feel?"

Jade sighed, knowing the minute she said the words it would be all over. Lincoln Donovan would have her heart once again. She hadn't wanted to take this plunge, to surrender her heart so quickly. But again, this was not a choice. His hips circled, he pulled back then thrust forth again and there wasn't a force on this earth strong enough to stop it.

"You make me feel cherished," she said, riding that glorious wave until it splashed and crashed with urgency against the shore. "And that scares me."

Linc heard her words but before he could process them completely he was overtaken. He plunged inside of her one last time before exploding.

Moonlight danced across the bed as Jade rolled over and rubbed her eyes. She'd been in a deep sleep, the kind that wakes you up to a feeling of disorientation. She wondered where she was then lifted a knee and felt the hardness of a male body beside her. He was lying on his side with his back facing her. It only took a second for her memory to come back. She'd slept with Linc. Again.

With a deep sigh she recalled how good it was. Again.

To her surprise he stirred then reached for her. When her head was settled on his chest and his arms wrapped tightly around her she sighed in contentment.

"Why didn't you tell me you owned a spa?"

His question came from out of the blue, startling her with a dose of reality. "It never came up."

"It did but you deliberately omitted it. Aren't you proud of your accomplishment?"

She was more than proud. She'd beat the odds and come out on top. She'd followed her dream and seen it to fruition. Of course she was proud. She just hadn't thought he'd care. "I didn't think it mattered either way to you."

His fingers massaged her scalp and he leaned forward to kiss her forehead. "You matter to me, Jade. You can tell me anything."

She thought about his words for a minute then decided he was simply speaking in the afterglow of lovemaking. He really didn't care to hear about her life.

"You can tell me why you were really at my casino. And before you do you should know that

I don't believe for one minute that you're irresponsible or foolish. The claim that you lost five thousand dollars that you can't afford to repay is not logical."

Damn, he'd picked a fine time to hit her with all this. But Jade felt a flood of relief. She wasn't good at all these stories and misconceptions. She prided herself on her honesty and her integrity. But these last few days she'd let herself down. "I have a younger sister who's impulsive and carefree. I'm the responsible one, the oldest and the caretaker. If you met Noelle I'm sure you'd have no problem placing the irresponsible cap on her head."

"Why—"

"My mother always told me to take care of Noelle," she interrupted him. "I got her up in the morning, made sure she washed and fed her breakfast. I combed her hair and helped her with her homework. I walked her to school and I picked her up in the afternoon. I've taken care of her all her life."

"That wasn't your job," Linc said sternly.

"It was my purpose. Mommy could barely take care of herself let alone two kids. My father left when Noelle was born. I was only two-and-a-half years old then. He broke Mommy's heart and only alcohol could mend it."

"Jade, I'm so sorry."

He'd opened the door and now things that she

hadn't spoken about in years came pouring out. "It was only a temporary mend though. Mommy died when I was sixteen. Noelle was fourteen and Grammy sent for us. We moved here to Las Vegas. But Grammy wasn't like Mommy. She taught us to be independent, to stand on our own feet, to pull our own weight. Somehow I don't think Noelle paid as much attention as I did."

"So it's Noelle's debt you're repaying?"

She nodded. "You don't have to say it. I know I can't keep bailing her out and I told her that this was the absolute last time. She's a grown woman and I don't have time to continue taking care of her."

"I'm glad to hear that. But I feel like an ass now for making you repay a debt that was never yours." He took a deep breath. "We should call this off."

Jade sat up so quickly a wave of dizziness hit and she had to wait a moment before she spoke. "No!" She turned to him and steadied her breathing. "I mean, I told Noelle I would handle this one last problem for her. I can't go back on my word. Besides, she doesn't have the money to pay you back. I have more money than she does. And I do not want my sister to go to jail."

Linc lifted a hand to smooth down her straying hair. "I won't have your sister thrown in jail, Jade. But it's not fair that you're taking the fall for her.

It's not fair that you're here against your will because of her."

"I'm not." She loved the feel of his hands in her hair. "Here against my will, I mean."

He smiled up at her. "Now you're not. But a few hours ago you were. You were doing a job, working off a debt that's not yours. Your sister is grown. She should be handling her own business."

Her gaze fell from his momentarily. "I know. She wasn't thrilled to hear about our little arrangement so I think she's feeling a little guilt now."

"Why wasn't she thrilled? You're fixing her problem, something I presume you do for her a lot."

"I do it too much. But that's not what she had a problem with. She knew how hard spending a week with you would be for me."

His hand had fallen to her shoulders and now the small of her back where he traced little circles, slowly, repeatedly. Her bones turning to mush with each passing second.

"And has it been hard for you?"

She looked at him and couldn't help but smile. He was so handsome and so tempting. She stroked his cheek and prayed that the love swelling inside her for him wasn't written all over her face. "You were a part of my life that needed to be reconciled. I needed to know why you'd left."

"And now you do."

She nodded. "Yes. Now I do."

They were silent.

He pulled her down on top of him, hugging her tightly, inhaling the scent of her hair. "Do me a favor?"

Anything, she wanted to say but instead said, "What?"

"Make love to me one more time before you go."

Jade didn't speak but lifted up from him. She reached to the nightstand and plucked a foil packet from the box he'd discarded last night. Taking his already erect penis into her hands she slipped the condom on him.

He sucked in a breath but was otherwise quiet.

She straddled him keeping her eyes on him as she slid slowly down onto his shaft. His hands came to her hips and he gripped her.

"Thank you," he whispered then thrust his hips up into her to seal their joining.

Blissful sensations moved through her and she bit her bottom lip to keep from crying out. "Don't thank me. My job's not finished yet."

Then they found a rhythm and no further words were spoken. The only sound echoing in the room was that of satisfied lovers finding their mutual release through a sensual dance as old as time.

* * *

Beside him she slept, silent and content, words he never thought he'd use to describe Jade Vincent. She had the type of personality that made anybody like her. She was smart. She was spirited. She was caring and conscientious. And she was damned pretty—animated at times and pigheaded at others. She was a variety of things all rolled into one very attractive package.

The most recent trait he could add to her repertoire was loyal. He was still trying to get his mind around the fact that she'd agreed to this week with him to save her sister. His thoughts on that matter were conflicted. On the one hand he was angry with her sister for being selfish enough to let her agree to something like this to save her ass. On the other hand, he was glad her sister was irresponsible enough to lose the money, otherwise he would most likely have never run into Jade again.

Still, it wasn't right. She wasn't here of her own free will. Even though he'd offered to release her from the deal she'd refused, stating that she'd given her word and she wanted her sister's slate wiped clean. She loved her sister an awful lot, there was no question about that. But was her sister worthy of that love? He was determined to find out.

Chapter 8

Linc was late for breakfast. He'd left Jade still sleeping in the bed and gone to the den to make a few calls.

By the time he entered the dining room everyone was talking and enjoying the meal. Everyone except Jade, that is. This was unusual and he was sure he wasn't the only one who noticed it.

"The party wasn't the same after you and Jade left, Lincoln."

"I'm sorry about that," Linc said honestly. "But we had some things to discuss."

"And did you…discuss things?" Trent asked.

Linc took his question to mean what they'd spoken about yesterday at the pool, about him looking into Jade's background. And while he'd initiated his own investigation, he knew all he needed to know about Jade's background. But again, these were things Trent did not need to know. "Yes. Everything is resolved." He turned to her for support. "Isn't that right, Jade?"

She looked up from her plate. "Yes. Everything is resolved." She smiled and his gut clenched.

Showering and dressing alone this morning gave him time to think about how things had changed between them. He was first to admit that sleeping with her again had, in fact, changed the dynamics of their relationship. But it was changing before then. He felt closer to her now than he ever had to anyone in his life. He wondered how she felt about their situation now. He still hadn't gotten the chance to talk about making it more permanent but he'd get to that after he took care of a few other things.

"So we're heading into town for a day of sight-seeing. I've rented a motor coach for everyone who doesn't want to drive," Beverly told them.

Jade seemed thankful for the change of conversation. "That sounds like fun."

For unknown reasons Linc tensed. "Actually, I already made plans for us." He was used to making plans and calling the shots.

Jade looked at him questioningly. He wasn't used to having those shots questioned, by anyone. Still he could see her mind trying to figure out why they wouldn't be going on the family outing. Last night she'd told him that she was still staying partly because of the deal she'd made on her sister's behalf and partly because she didn't want him to have to answer his family's obvious questions. So their deal was still on. She was still staying for the week. And that still wasn't long enough for him.

"Really? What are you two lovebirds doing today?" Henry asked.

Linc hesitated, not sure he wanted everybody to know about the day he had planned. But then her eyes found his again and the urge to do whatever he could to make her happy overwhelmed him. "We're going to spend some quality time together." He spoke in a tone that dared anyone to comment and since his family knew him so well, they didn't.

The dining room cleared shortly after that declaration. Then they were alone.

"Hey, beautiful," he said from across the table.

A slow smile spread across her face. "Hey, yourself."

This time there was no doubt that her smile was just for him and that fact warmed him. "So, you ready to get started with our day?"

"I thought we were supposed to be keeping up the pretense for your family."

Linc remained quiet for a moment. "A loving couple would undoubtedly want some time to themselves, right?"

"I guess they would."

He rose and came to stand beside her. "I just want to spend the day with you. Alone. Is that okay with you?"

The smile she gave him this time put all others to shame and he found himself smiling equally as broad.

"That's just fine with me," she said, taking the hand he'd offered. "So, what do you have planned?"

"It's supposed to be a beautiful day, ninety-two degrees. It's a perfect beach day if you ask me."

She frowned. "Is there a beach around here?"

Unable to resist touching her again Linc rubbed his knuckles over the soft skin of her cheek. "No. And that really bothered my mother when they purchased the land. So much so that Dad made one for her."

Jade looked incredulous. "Really?"

"Yes. My mother loves the beach so he built her one."

She sighed. "That's so sweet."

"You think so?" His hand moved to her hair. He loved touching her.

"Yes. It is."

"I'll have to ask him for some tips on sweet things to do." And then because they were so close and she was so alluring, he dropped a soft kiss on her lips.

"I missed you this morning."

"Then how come you were gone when I woke up?"

"I had some things to take care of. I wanted to make sure I was completely free for the day with you."

She tilted her head as she looked up at him. "That's sweet."

Her words were music to his ears and going right along with his plans. He wanted to get their day going then realized there was one more thing he needed to handle first. "We'll spend the day on the beach, getting to know each other better. It'll be fun."

Jade's eyes sparkled, just the way he liked to see them. "Yes. It'll be fun," she said.

"I just have one call to make and I'll be ready to go." He held her in a loose embrace and yet his blood had already begun to warm.

"I thought you said you took care of everything earlier."

"I did, but there's just one phone call that can't
wait until tomorrow."

"Okay. I'll go to the kitchen to see about
getting us a picnic lunch. Then I'll change and be
ready."

"Great. I'll only be about fifteen minutes." He
kissed her again for good measure then left the
room with a pep in his step he couldn't remember
having before.

Almost an hour had passed and Jade had
secured their lunch and changed her clothes. But
Linc was nowhere to be found.

That was just as well because it gave her a little
time to get her thoughts together. Last night had
surpassed all the dreams she'd ever had. Linc had
been more than she'd remembered. Then he'd
asked her about her business and her life and she'd
told him what he needed to know. She'd told him
about Noelle and her real reason for being here.
And he, to her surprise, had offered her a way out.

Now in the light of day she realized she should
have taken that way out. The mere fact that he
offered it could only mean that she was disposable
to him. But she'd been caught up in the euphoria
of their lovemaking and she'd thought of the deal

she made. If she wasn't known for anything else in this life, she'd be known for keeping her word. So she was staying.

That meant she needed to make another difficult choice.

Picnic basket in hand she climbed the stairs to check their suite one last time. Although what she had to tell him would be difficult, butterflies danced in her stomach as she thought of spending the afternoon with Linc. She could go up these stairs and tell him right now. She could say it and be done with it. But he'd planned a day at the beach. She didn't want to totally spoil his plans.

"I thought you said half an hour." Dropping her picnic basket to the floor Jade walked toward him and stood while he looked at some papers on his desk. "You really do work too much, Linc. This beach thing was your idea and you haven't even changed yet," she exclaimed.

"I know. And I'm just finishing up."

She waved a hand toward the papers. "They'll be here when we get back. You were supposed to be getting into your swimsuit." She crossed the room to his closet and swung it open, only to find it full of suits, dress shirts and slacks. He really needed to relax more. Even the two pair of jeans he had were starched and draped over a hanger.

"I can find my own clothes, Jade."

He sounded amused but she was on a roll and wasn't about to leave him to the task again. "Sure you can but once you've started working your mind gets distorted." She pulled open a drawer and moved things aside until she found what she was looking for. With trunks in hand she turned to face him.

A seductive grin spread over his face. "Will you dress me too?"

Stuffy business clothes or not he was still gorgeous and he was headed directly for her. A tingle of warmth and a lick of growing excitement fizzled in her belly. In an attempt to suppress her wayward thoughts she responded in what she thought was an appropriate manner. "Do you want me to?" Touching him again would be heaven. It would be dangerous and it would undoubtedly stall their trip to the beach, but it would certainly be worth it.

He stood directly in front of her now, large as life and sexy as hell. He didn't move but waggled his brows, reducing her insides to jelly. Only he had the power to do that.

"Unless you're afraid to dress me."

Her lips tightened. He was incorrigible. And she, as he well knew, could not resist a challenge. Reaching up she loosened his tie, pulled it free from his neck and let it fall to the floor. Her hands slid over the broad expanse of his chest before settling on the buttons of his shirt.

Linc watched her closely while she comman-
deered his clothing, not moving a muscle. Jade's
heart thumped in her chest. Through his shirt she
felt the hardened ridges of his chest and remembered kissing him there. "Once we get you into
something a little more suitable we can hit the
beach," she said in a shaky voice.

"I'm not sure we're going to make it to the
beach," he said through clenched teeth.

The power she held was irresistible and she let
her nails scrape over his now bare chest. "Now I
know you have more control than that, Lincoln."

He sucked in a breath and caught her wrists.
"You test my control."

Just as he shattered hers, she thought with
rising desire. "I apologize. I'll keep my mind on
the business at hand from now on." She hastily
moved to his pants and had him completely undressed in seconds. Thrusting his trunks toward
him she looked down at his marvelous erection.
"You might want to do a little less concentrating
yourself," she said and skirted around him.

Her throat was tight with the pain of being
close to him. They'd been intimate and it showed.
In the way he looked at her and in the way that
he talked to her. It was apparent that they were
lovers.

But was that all he intended them to be?

* * *

Linc parked the car and came around to open her door for her. She stepped out and was about to go around to the trunk for the picnic basket when he cupped her chin and tilted her head to look at him. "I'm sorry," he said sincerely.

The sunlit sky was a brilliant backdrop to his chiseled good looks. Even with her new resignation she was not immune. She licked her lips nervously. "Sorry for what?"

He tucked a strand of hair behind her ear. "For leaving you eight years ago. I was selfish and stupid. I hurt you and for that I can't apologize enough."

If she thought his words caught her off guard then the kiss he laid on her could have stopped the world from turning. It was different than the other kisses they'd shared, softer, sweeter and definitely more potent. His lips were barely touching hers, then his tongue was stroking slowly, sinuously over hers, taking complete possession of her mouth and her senses.

He wasn't making this easy. Here she was prepared for a knock-down, drag-out round of renegotiation of their terms and he was charming the pants off her.

"Come," he said when he finally broke the kiss. "The beach is this way."

Her legs felt like molded Jell-O but she managed to follow him down a slope and through a brush of trees. Her breath caught as the sound of a waterfall echoed from the distance. White sand stretched for about five miles before falling into a circle of crystal-clear water. Never had she seen such a sight in Las Vegas. It was a secluded spot. A spot for lovers. And she was there with Linc.

"Let's sit over there." With the picnic basket in one hand and her hand firmly in the other Linc led her to a small spot near a huge tree offering shade. If she really concentrated she could dismiss this feeling of elation spreading throughout her body. At best, she could convince herself that it was simply a product of lovemaking afterglow, or his way of seducing her into another night. Both of which she was probably going to fall for. Still, his touch was gentle, his words sweet and her heart way too vulnerable.

He put the picnic basket down then flipped it open to pull out a beach blanket. He chuckled as he pulled out another one of her shopping spree purchases. "Tweety Bird? We're sitting on a Tweety Bird blanket?"

That had actually been a whimsical find, one she hadn't planned on him actually seeing. But when he brought up the day at the beach she knew it would be perfect for lounging with its thick fleece material. "Yup, I have a Tweety Bird fetish."

He gave her a smoldering look. "There's nothing wrong with a fetish."

She looked away as he spread the blanket out. His eyes were different today, like dark windows to his innermost thoughts. She could get lost in those eyes and in this man. And realized with a start that she was already headed down that road. The realist part of her wanted to keep her distance, to preserve her heart. But her heart wanted her to take the plunge and either sink or swim.

"Do you have suntan lotion in here?" he spoke from behind her.

Taking a deep breath she turned. "Sure do." Sinking down to her knees she leaned over the picnic basket and retrieved the tube.

Linc almost groaned. She might as well just ditch the shorts—they weren't doing anything to cover body parts too enticing to be displayed. It's a damn good thing they were on a private beach or he'd spend most of the day fighting off the men bold enough to stare at her.

"You want me to put some on you?" she asked when she'd returned to a sitting position beside him.

"No. I want to put some on you." He took the bottle from her hands and flipped the top open, needing desperately to get his hands on her.

"That's not necessary. I put some on already," she told him.

"The sun is scorching today. I wouldn't want you to burn." He poured a generous portion in his hand. "Turn around," he instructed.

She took a moment to consider his words then acquiesced. "Okay, I guess a little more couldn't hurt." She turned so that her back faced him.

Rising up on his knees Linc gently smoothed the cool lotion onto her warm skin—soft and tempting didn't begin to describe it. His fingers moved over her shoulder blades, slowly inching down. Lifting the thin strap of her top, he covered her middle back, gradually massaging down her spine and over her rib cage. Squeezing more lotion into his hand, his jaw clenched as he moved farther down her torso until brushing the rim of her shorts.

"Wait a second." Jade jumped up and quickly discarded the shorts.

Linc reined in every bit of control he possessed. The thinnest slip of ice-blue material rode low on her hips and across the most delectable bottom he had ever seen. What happened to the modest dark blue number she'd worn before? Jade lay across the blanket this time and he shifted so that he could get the backs of her legs. He wasn't going to venture near the part of her anatomy that had his blood pumping thick and hot in his veins. Not yet, anyway. They had all day.

When he was finished with her backside he instructed her to turn over. Sweet torture, were the only words capable of describing what he was putting himself through. But he wouldn't trade it for all the tea in China. He marveled over every inch of smooth, creamy skin that his fingers came in contact with. He lifted one of her arms, languorously rubbing the lotion into every crevice. Her eyes had been closed but as his hand moved up her arm his fingers brushed against her breast and they quickly opened.

Hazel eyes turned dark as his hand stilled. Holding her gaze, Linc turned his hand from her arm to trace the outline of her bikini top with his fingertip. She didn't move. Linc sucked in his breath and since she hadn't made a move to either stop or berate him, let his finger slip beneath the material of her top grazing her nipple.

Jade did move then. "Maybe I should put some lotion on you." She sat up, grabbing the bottle of lotion, pouring a generous amount into her small hands.

Linc didn't argue, mostly because he couldn't find the words to speak. He turned his back to her thinking that he would be safe now. Touching her was intimate, erotic and pulled him closer to ravishing her out here on the open beach. The change between them was now more evident. His mind, while trained to focus on the delectable sight before him, was now giving way to his heart, to the incessant murmurings of what was building there.

His first instinct was to deny it, to fight whatever it was she'd done to him. Making love to her had been sweet, a memory he wanted to relive over and over again as frequently as possible.

Jade was still flushed and completely turned on by Linc's touch. She thought she could handle the simple application of suntan lotion, not realizing it could be so erotic, so sensually devastating. But at Linc's first touch she'd known she'd been mistaken. His hands had moved over her with such gentle strokes that she'd simply given in to the arousal blooming inside. Her skin still tingled from his touch and longed for more.

Now, she thought she was about to give him a dose of his own medicine. She couldn't wait to get her hands on him, to tease his senses the way he'd done her. To apply just a small amount of torture and see where they ended up.

She squirted the lotion into her palm then put her hands together to warm the solution. With long, easy strokes, similar to the ones used in a therapeutic massage, she moved over his back marveling at the shiny coat she'd added to his dark skin. Moving her thumbs up and down his spine her fingers grazed his ribcage and she felt him begin to relax.

"How much do you charge for this type of torture?" he asked.

"An hour of therapeutic massage is eighty dollars." She poured more lotion into her hands and lifted one of his arms. She gripped his biceps, rubbing the lotion into the turgid muscle.

"How many different types of massages are there?"

"Are you thinking of trying them all?"

"I'm thinking of trying anything that will keep your hands on me."

She smiled and moved to the other arm. He had strong hands and while it wasn't quite necessary she applied lotion to them, too, taking special care with each finger as she did. She felt the strength in those hands and remembered them on her.

"What else would you like to try?" she asked, curious as to what thoughts were going through his mind. She was perfectly aware of where her torrid thoughts were headed.

"With you? Everything," he said simply.

She couldn't stifle a smile. "Not with me, silly. I mean in life. You said you always knew you wanted to open a casino. Well, you've done that. What else would you like to do?"

He paused and she moved down to lotion the backs of his thighs. She straddled one leg at a time loving the feel of his muscles against her skin. Linc was a gorgeous male specimen, one she hungered for.

"I've been thinking of working on my personal life. It gets a little lonely in that penthouse at night."

"How could you possibly be lonely when you live in a casino? You are constantly surrounded by people. And then you have your family when you tire of strangers. Some people would say you have it all."

Linc turned over, taking his time so as not to send her sprawling over the blanket. He stared up at her and she grasped the bottle of suntan lotion. His gaze was heated, almost indecent, but his words were surprisingly calm.

"Do you think I have it all?"

"I think..." She licked her lips. "I think that you have a pretty good life from where I'm standing."

"I thought that too for a while. But lately I've been feeling incomplete."

"Really?" She'd felt incomplete for the last eight years.

"You missed this side." He nodded down at his chest.

She was shifting quickly between her physical reaction to him and the emotions he'd been stirring since last night. She had to get a grip or he'd think she was as kooky as the girls at that dorm party eight years ago. "No, I didn't. I was waiting for you to finish talking."

He smiled and her bikini bottom became damp. She was fighting a losing battle.

With her hands well-lathered with lotion she moved to his chest and leaned over awkwardly to apply it.

He grasped her by the hips and lifted her to straddle him. "You'll get better coverage this way."

Better coverage and a better feel for why her temperature had risen a few notches. "That I will." She sighed then placed her hands over his chest and rubbed. He sat up straight, leafing his fingers through her hair as she applied the lotion more thoroughly.

"I always thought you had lovely hair," he said absently.

She prayed her heart wouldn't beat right out of her chest then chanced a look at him. "The first time I saw you I thought you should be on the cover of a sports magazine."

"I played football in high school but in college I focused more on academics."

"I like a man with brains."

His fingers splayed over her hips and down to her bottom.

"What else do you like?"

Now that was a loaded question and one she couldn't answer because heat was soaring through her veins, pooling in her center to the point that she seriously contemplated stripping and taking him right here and now. The sound of cascading water not too far in the distance was a welcome solution, one she didn't intend to pass up.

She slapped her hands to his chest then stood. "Race you in," she challenged.

Linc looked up at her. Gloriously long, perfectly shaped legs led to the small wisp of light-blue material draping low on her hips. The small indentation of her navel, her flat stomach, the curve of her breasts jutting forward covered in the same light-blue material, nipples puckered so that they poked through like tiny stars twinkling seductively at him. He swallowed hard then mustering all his strength, stood. "See ya!" he yelled before taking off down the beach.

Jade yelped and ran behind him.

The water was cool against his heated skin as he wadded in deeper until it came to his chest. In one swift motion he submerged himself, hoping, but knowing instinctively that it would not cool

him off. Jade in that skimpy bathing suit, Jade
with her hands all over him, Jade straddling him
and looking at him with desire so openly visible
in her eyes had his whole body ablaze. When he
resurfaced, he dragged his hand over his face and
opened his eyes. Water splashed over his face
quickly and repeatedly. He shook his head trying
to catch his breath.

"You big cheater!" Jade yelled as she continued to splash him.

He laughed and walked toward the flailing
woman, grabbing her around the waist. "I didn't
cheat. You're just slow." Pulling her closer he
looked down into her smiling face, her sparkling
eyes, and felt a grip around his heart. Her lips
curved into a smile as her arms circled around his
neck. God, he wanted to kiss her right now. He
wanted to hold her in his arms and keep her safe,
keep her happy.

With a firm grip on her waist, he lifted her so
that her feet no longer touched the ground. She
gasped, her mouth opening slightly. Her lips
hovered scant inches above his as he let her body
slide down the length of his, until they were perfectly aligned.

When his lips finally touched hers everything
else ceased to exist. His arms tightened around her

as he nibbled on her lower lip. The soft skin swelled in his mouth and he hungered for more. Extending his tongue he ran it across the inside of her lip. She moaned, her arms tightening, pulling his head closer.

He took her top lip between his teeth, biting down lightly as she dragged her tongue across his bottom lip. All the blood drained from his head, finding a nice warm spot at his groin. Tilting his head, he opened his mouth and plunged, offering her a part of himself he'd never offered any woman before.

For a minute he felt her hesitate and panicked. But then she opened her mouth in response, her tongue mingling fiercely with his. He held her tightly letting his tongue lavish the contours of her mouth, his hands running up and down her back. When her legs wrapped around his waist he groaned into her mouth, pulling her closer—if that were possible. His hands cupped her bottom, holding her tightly as his mind decided that he would never let her go.

Jade rubbed her throbbing center against the rim of his boxers even though she knew it was a mistake. He was delectably hard as she lowered herself so that his erection passed directly over her opening. His kiss was persistent, his tongue delving deeper and deeper until he almost swallowed her whole.

Water splashed from the stream splattering them in cool drops, effectively bringing her out of her erotic haze but thrusting her into a romantic bliss. She tore her lips away from Linc's even though he continued to hold her in the circle of his arms. Jade opened her eyes, the sky and waterline swirling in the distance. When she was able to focus on him, on the deep brown of his eyes, the chiseled outline of his face and the desire that was so perfectly clear, she slid down his body, passing that awesome arousal as it now pressed against her stomach.

"I never imagined being like this with you again." She'd dreamed it but she'd never been a believer of dreams coming true, especially not where Lincoln Donovan was concerned.

"Do you like it?" He ground his hips against her.

"I like it very much."

In a flash his hand was beneath the rim of her bikini bottom pushing the slip of material down her legs. "Then show me."

She didn't give it another thought but linked her arms around his neck and hoisted her legs around his waist, locking them at his back. The water made her almost weightless but with Linc's strength she knew that whether they were under water or on ground he would have still been able to rid himself of the trunks keeping her in place at the same time. "How's this?"

He smiled, kissed her quickly, his tongue dipping into her mouth momentarily. He shifted then slipped his arousal deeply into her. "That is perfect."

Chapter 9

"We should talk about last night. And just now."
She lay on her back on top of the Tweety blanket
naked. Her bikini top had been tossed to the side
when they'd come from the water. Her bottom
she assumed was still in the water.

This was not how she'd planned to tell him.
Things had happened quickly between them and
she'd been too weak or too aroused to stop it.
Now, however, her resolve was back.

Linc lay on his back, too. Reaching between
them he took her hand in his. "Last night was
very special to me, Jade. You are special to me. I
hope you know that."

Not quite special enough since he hadn't said he loved her. It was funny how desperately she'd wanted him to say that. Even just a few minutes ago she'd felt the change between them, felt the close-ness grow and connect. But he hadn't said the words.

That proved beyond any doubt that what she was about to do was for the best. The bottom line was that the next man Jade willingly gave her heart to would have to be worthy. He would be ready to commit to her without a second thought. She would have no fear that he was going to break her heart. Linc could not actively participate in a relationship, he'd told her so himself.

He'd said he was selfish and self-centered. She wondered if those were the real reasons. These last few days she hadn't seen either of those traits in him. At any rate, he didn't want a commitment and she wasn't willing to accept anything less.

"I enjoyed myself, too, Linc. But what I mean is, well…" Where were the words? Her mind was totally blank. Especially with him touching her.

"Take your time, baby. I'm not going anywhere."

His words gripped her heart like a vice and she wanted to cry out in pain. Instead she remained focused, her gaze skyward. Big, puffy white clouds dotted the blue background. She could lose herself in those clouds. Then she wouldn't have to deal with the here and now. She wouldn't have to deal with her feelings for Linc. But that was cowardly and she wasn't about to go out like that.

So she took a deep breath and recited the words she'd worked on this morning. "Last night was really nice, but we both know it's not smart to let it happen again. I understand that I am still technically in your employ and that at this point it's pretty much voluntary. But I'm not backing out of our deal. I just want to add a few stipulations to our agreement."

Linc sat up then and stared down at her. "Excuse me?"

"I'd like to revise our agreement. Specifically the sleeping arrangements."

He quirked a brow at her and she acknowledged then that she was totally nude and so was he. This wasn't the ideal situation to be having this conversation but it was either now or never for her. Self-preservation had to prevail over embarrassment or even arousal this time.

"From now until the end of this week I will sleep alone. You can either sleep on the couch or the floor, it's your choice. And there will be no more touching." He was watching her intently and she grew even more uncomfortable. Pulling her hand out of his she searched the bag for her shorts and slipped them on. Then she found her top and put that on, too.

All the while Linc watched her not saying a word. The fact that he hadn't responded gave her more time to gather their things, to gather her strength. She knew Linc. At least she now knew him better than she had before. He wasn't going to let this rest. He wasn't going to accept it easily. But she would be stronger. She would walk away whole this time. That's what she'd promised herself the first day she'd agreed to this arrangement.

"You can't change things now," he said quietly.

So quietly she almost didn't hear him. But she turned and he was sitting there staring at her. "Yes. I can." He didn't understand how much she had to do this.

"What's really going on, Jade? Are we back to that social status thing because I thought we went over that last night."

"You said you didn't think of me as being in a different class from you. I believe that's not what you think. But that doesn't change the facts. At any rate, that's not why I'm suggesting the change."

"Then what is the reason? Is it about last night? Because I didn't leave—"

His voice trailed off but she finished the sentence for him. "No. You didn't leave me this time. At least not for good."

He dragged a hand down his face. "Jade, I've apologized for that."

She nodded. "And I accept your apology. But it doesn't take the pain away."

"Then how can I take the pain away? I can't change the past so tell me what I can do to make the present better?"

She desperately wanted to tell him. But she knew it wouldn't matter. "There's nothing you can do, Linc. It's just something I have to deal with. Besides, the agreement was for a week. We're two mature adults. Surely we can go the next three days without touching each other. Without being with each other."

"What happens if I don't agree?"

"Then I'll leave."

"What about the debt?"

She stiffened. "I told you in the beginning that my body was not for sale."

Linc had physically flinched when she said those words. Did she really think he was paying for her to sleep with him? Well, wasn't he?

He was confused. Everything she was saying was coming out of left field. He thought that for once in their history together they were on the same page. Last night had been incredible, so much so that he couldn't wait to be alone with her today. And today had been incredible. How come she didn't feel the same?

"You can't leave."

"I can and I will if my stipulations aren't met," she said adamantly.

Linc clenched his teeth and stared at her then relaxed as he realized what she was really doing. "Are you going to punish every man for what he did?"

Her eyes widened. "What are you talking about?"

"Charles Benson. You were supposed to marry him but he abandoned you. Are you really still angry with me or am I taking the punishment for him?"

She looked confused and hurt. "I…" she began, closed her eyes and took a deep breath. "He has nothing to do with this."

"Doesn't he? You wouldn't have been in my casino if he hadn't stolen your money."

She gasped. "How did you know that? Did you have me investigated? How dare you!" she raged.

"Calm down. It wasn't like that," he said when she was about to go off again. "I investigated you like I would investigate any new employee and because I knew that you weren't telling me the whole story. I wanted to help."

"So you slept with me? Knowing what I'd just

been through you seduced me anyway. How honorable of you."

Linc swore. No matter what he did or said she was determined to think the worst of him. He figured it was the price he had to pay for helping sour her against men. But this had gone on long enough. He cared about her now, surely she had to realize that.

He grabbed her shoulders, pulling her hard against his chest. "I slept with you because I wanted you. *You* slept with *me* because you wanted me, too." When she didn't respond he loosened his grip on her and brushed a hand over her cheek. "I've apologized for what I did eight years ago. There's nothing more I can do about that. But I can't make amends for another man's mistakes."

She'd been watching him intently, her eyes filling with tears. Tears that undid him completely. Again he swore and let out a deep breath. He'd never had to force a woman to sleep with him and he wouldn't start now. If this was what she wanted then this was what she'd get. "I'll accept your stipulations regarding the sleeping arrangements. But I won't stop touching you."

To further prove his point he traced a finger over her cheek. "I can't stop touching you."

Her tears came freely then and Linc held her

as she purged herself, whispering into her hair, "I'm sorry that he hurt you."

She shuddered against him and he held her tighter. She was so strong, so independent. She wouldn't have allowed herself to hurt before because there was nobody to ease that pain for her. But he was here now.

His anger toward Charles Benson formed a fiery ball in the pit of his stomach and he knew instinctively how to soothe this pain for Jade, how to make her whole again.

Linc and Jade walked through the front door of the house hand in hand. Again, the dynamics between them had shifted. Jade felt weary of the emotional turmoil and wanted only to claim some time to be alone to think. She'd agreed to stay with Linc for the duration of the week. There wasn't much choice in that matter. And Linc had agreed to her stipulations, sort of. Now she needed time to adjust to their new standing, time to strengthen herself for the days ahead.

But her bad luck struck again.

"Lincoln! I've been waiting for you," a high-pitched voice sounded upon their entrance.

Jade recognized the voice before she looked in the direction from which it came and her insides boiled. Hadn't she dealt with this woman yesterday? Was she really that dense that she hadn't picked up the hint?

"Hello, Leslie. I wasn't expecting to see you today," Linc said in what Jade surmised as a pleasant tone.

Leslie Kindle wasted no time moving as close to Linc as she possibly could considering he was still holding Jade's hand. "I know. I just decided to stop by since we really didn't get a chance to finish talking yesterday."

With that the vixen had the audacity to toss Jade a searing look.

Damn. The last thing she felt like was putting somebody in their place but she would not be disrespected no matter how physically and mentally tired she was. "Good afternoon, Leslie. I see we still have a misunderstanding," Jade said tightly.

Linc squeezed her hand and spoke. "I'm sorry, Leslie, but I don't really have time to talk to you today, either."

"But Lincoln, you always make time for me." Leslie pushed up against Linc's left side, her voice lowering to a whining drawl that sent chills up Jade's spine. "Besides, I checked. There aren't any Vincents of importance around here." Peering around Linc, Leslie gave Jade a satisfied smile.

Jade wrenched her hand from Linc's and moved to stand in front of Leslie. "While you were checking you should have researched how many Vincents were known for kicking ass!"

"Oh, my!" Leslie cowered behind Linc. "You see, I was right. She has no breeding or class. You really shouldn't be wasting your time with her, Lincoln."

"I'll show you breeding and class." Jade swung wildly in the woman's direction but Linc had stepped between them, catching the blow against the back of his shoulder.

"Leslie, I think you should leave," Linc said, while holding Jade back.

"Leave? Me? Why should I leave? She's the one acting like a hood rat. But I guess we can't really blame her since that's all she knows."

Jade moved around Linc this time. He extended an arm to keep her from swinging at Leslie again but Jade only held a hand up in his direction. "Don't worry, I'm not going to hit the trick," she said in a slow, menacing tone. "She's not worth it. But know this, I may not be from your class and of your breeding but that's not my loss at all. I'd rather be the strong, independent woman I am instead of a lonely, conniving, desperate wench like you."

Linc moved his arm as Leslie gasped at Jade's words.

"Are you going to let her speak to me this way, Lincoln?" Leslie asked in outrage.

"*Lincoln—*" Jade mimicked Leslie's irritating voice "—does not control me or my actions. For your sake I'd advise you to steer clear of me and *Lincoln* for the duration of this week. Because the next time I might not be able to hold my hood rat tendencies in check."

With that said, Jade walked up the stairs to her room.

"There was no stipulation in our new arrangement that said we couldn't have a quiet dinner, alone," Linc countered when she'd argued against the dinner in their room later that evening.

Jade stewed over her own stupidity. She should have outlined specific activities and she should have stated that they could under no circumstances be alone together. Now, more than ever, it was imperative that she kept a level head where Linc was concerned. But a good businesswoman wouldn't go back to the negotiating table again on such a technicality so she sucked it up and gave him a stilted smile.

"You're absolutely right. There is no reason why we can't have dinner together. Alone." After her embarrassing bout with tears their beach outing had taken a better turn. While she'd been ready to leave, Linc insisted that they stay. After he'd dressed, they'd shared the lunch of shrimp salad sandwiches and fruit prepared by the cook and talked about their time in college. They'd had a lot in common back then. It was funny how they'd never got around to figuring that out.

Linc, as she'd already come to see during the week, was pleasant to be around, if you could handle the strong, arrogant type who, instead of admitting defeat, issued a challenge. It probably didn't help that she didn't like to admit defeat, either and relished a good challenge. That's why they'd arm wrestled for the last slice of watermelon and raced from one end of the beach to the other to see who would drive home since they were both stuffed with food and tired from the beaming sun.

He'd won and she wasn't happy about it but the chocolate sundae he'd brought her after they'd arrived in their room made up for it.

"I'm sure your mother won't be happy about us skipping dinner with them." She gave one last shot at getting out of more time alone with him.

"No good." He shook his head and smiled. "I suggested it to her and she thought it was an excellent idea. So you're stuck with me, like it or not."

She smiled because it wasn't such a hard thing to do around him. "Then I guess you're lucky that I like it."

"Excellent." He moved closer and lifted her hand to his lips, paused briefly, then kissed her.

"Before we eat I want to apologize." She decided it was best to get it over with.

Linc looked perplexed. "Apologize for what?"

"For the scene I created with Leslie Kindle. Don't get me wrong, I'm not sorry about what I said to her because she deserved it. But I shouldn't have gotten physical in your mother's house."

Linc chuckled. "I haven't seen a chick fight in years."

Jade couldn't help but laugh herself. "And I'm sure you miss them."

"It would have been interesting, that's for sure."

Jade groaned.

He touched her shoulders and looked at her seriously. "There's no need to apologize. If some dude was pushing up on you right in front of me I'd hit him and talk later, too. So it's cool. Besides, Leslie is irritating as hell."

"Yes. She is." Jade smiled. "But she had a point about the class thing."

Linc cut her off quickly. "No, she didn't, and I don't want you thinking that anymore. I don't care who you're related to, where you were born or how much money you have. If I wanted to spend the week with a high-society airhead I have plenty to choose from."

He cupped her face and dropped a soft kiss on her lips. "I chose you."

Jade found herself anticipating the contact and, despite her resolve, wanting more. "Let's eat," she said before she grew any weaker.

She walked through the entryway leading to the living area of their suite. The sight before her made her pause. In the middle of the floor was a table draped in white linen with two chairs and a bouquet of peach roses. The lights were dim and scented candles—sandalwood if she wasn't mistaken—were all over the place. She closed her eyes and inhaled.

Linc came up behind her but didn't touch her, his lips close to her ear. "It's for relaxation, correct? I figured since you were into massage therapy, aromatherapy was a given. The sweet, exotic smell is meant to warm the senses."

And coupled with the man drive her absolutely bonkers! "Mmm-hmm." She felt his closeness seconds before his arms brushed her shoulders and her eyes settled on the sterling silver chain being positioned around her neck. With a gasp she touched her hand to the heart-shaped pendant in the center.

"I told you I'd get it fixed," Linc said as he clasped it at her neck.

Jade stared down at the necklace, her heart

filling with an emotion she didn't want to name. "But…it's not the same. I mean, you changed it," she whispered.

Linc moved around to stand in front of her. He looked down at the necklace then up into her eyes. "You said that it was a gift from your grand-mother. I could see how much it made you happy when you thought of her. So I figured if I put my own special touch on it, it would make you happy when you thought of me."

She looked away from him, afraid she'd cry again. What was with these pesky tears lately? Rubbing her fingers over the now diamond encir-cled heart she did feel happy thinking of him, thinking that he'd gone out of his way to do this for her. Carefully and with the effort of ten men tugging at her emotions she smiled up at him. "Thank you."

Linc smiled and her knees buckled.

"Have a seat." He motioned toward the table.

She groaned inwardly. Just looking at him in the dim light standing tall and handsome as a Greek god made her stomach perform a slow, very torturous somersault.

Unsure of what to say and rattled beyond reason Jade took a seat then leaned forward to smell the flowers. "I love peach roses."

"Really? I would have never guessed." He sat across from her, a small smile tugging at his lips.

"Who told you? Adam or your mother? They're the only two I've talked to enough to have let something that personal slip."

"You can talk to me about personal things too, Jade."

His tone was sincere. Actually he sounded a little hurt that she hadn't shared anything personal with him. But she had. She'd told him about Noelle but only because he'd asked. Most importantly, she'd shared herself. "That's not a part of our arrangement."

"I'd like to think that when the arrangement is over and done with we can still talk and be friends." He cleared his throat.

If he'd reached inside her chest and squeezed her heart personally, it couldn't have been more painful. His words only confirmed her reasoning behind the new stipulations. "Of course we can be friends," she lied. There was no use telling him that once she left this house on Sunday morning she had no intention of ever looking back, of ever thinking about Lincoln Donovan and his perfect family again.

He poured wine and they exchanged small talk.

She fixed their plates and they ate in companionable silence.

He stood and moved to the balcony they hadn't used until tonight. She remained seated until he sent a questioning glance prompting her to join him.

There was a light breeze when she stepped out beneath the indigo sky. Stars sprinkled the dark backdrop like confetti and she couldn't help but smile.

"You're too easy to please," he said.

"What gave you that idea?"

"Roses, candles and starlight. You look happy, content. I like that."

He wasn't being sweet, he was simply noticing the obvious, she told herself. "Then I guess you're right. I'm not difficult."

"No. Just stubborn."

She chuckled. "Grammy used to say that, too."

He moved closer until their arms touched. "Tell me about her."

Jade sucked in a gulp of night air and smiled. "My grandmother, Victoria Vincent. She passed away nine months ago." No matter how much time passed she still felt a pang of grief when she admitted that Grammy was gone.

"I'm sorry that she's gone."

"Gone but not forgotten." Jade tapped a hand over her heart. "I carry her with me here at all times. For so long she was all I had and now…" She broke off, looked away because she was afraid she'd cry again.

"And now you feel like you're alone."

She shook her head. "I know I'm not technically alone. I have Noelle. But I just needed her so much. And Linc, I miss her so much."

"It's not a crime to need someone, Jade. In fact, that's a part of being in a relationship."

She looked up at him, surprised that he'd said that. "What would you know about being in a relationship? You said you couldn't actively participate in one, remember?"

"That was when I was nineteen years old. Besides, my parents are good role models. They need each other and they don't make any qualms about admitting that fact."

"Yeah, your parents have a great marriage."

"Do you want to be married someday?" he asked.

"Nah." She shrugged. "I don't think I'm marriage material."

"That's ridiculous. Any man would be lucky to have you for his wife."

Any man but you, she silently filled in the gap. "Obviously not."

"Let me guess, you can't find anybody who meets your standards."

She frowned at that. "I don't have high standards for a mate. In fact, my goals are simple and to the point."

"And what are they?"

"You don't need to know," she said and continued to look out into the dark of night.

"Come on, if I were Adam or my mother you wouldn't have a problem telling me. You said we're friends and friends share things, so just tell me."

What the hell, he couldn't fill her qualifications, anyway. "I want the fairytale. I want the white knight to sweep me off my feet. I want him to be so in love with me he can't think straight. I want him to promise me the world even if it's just to make me feel better. Can you understand that?"

He smiled at her. "I can. But do you really think you'll find that? I mean, is there any room for something a little less heroic than your expectations?"

"No." She looked at him seriously. "Because that's what I deserve."

Chapter 10

Jade slept alone and awakened feeling a keen sense of loss. She knew it was her fault. She was the one to come up with the stipulations, and now she had to deal with them. After showering and dressing she'd gone into the sitting area of their room expecting to see Linc at his desk. But he wasn't there.

Blankets were still on the sofa where he'd obviously slept, but the man was nowhere in sight. With purposeful steps she went downstairs and straight to the dining room where everyone usually gathered for breakfast.

Today must have been her day to be shocked because the huge table looked utterly solemn. While it was still full of food, fine china and steaming coffee, it lacked one key ingredient: people.

"Good morning, dear. It's just you and I this morning," Beverly said as she buttered a croissant.

Jade pulled out a chair and sat. "Where is everyone?" she asked when she was really only concerned with the whereabouts of one person.

Beverly looked her way with an arched eyebrow. "Henry's with his horses. Adam had a date last night which I'm sure will keep him occupied until later this evening. Trent's in the den working on a case. And—" she paused took a bite of her croissant and savored it.

Jade poured a cup of coffee realizing just what the woman was doing and refusing to hang on her every word. With an inward chuckle she realized she liked Beverly Donovan a lot more than she'd anticipated.

When she was finished chewing Beverly dabbed a napkin at the corners of her mouth. "Lincoln said something about an emergency at the casino."

"The casino?" Jade paused, her coffee cup just inches from her lips. "So he's not here?"

"He had to return to Las Vegas. But he said he'll be back in the morning."

He went back to Vegas and hadn't bothered to tell her. She couldn't pinpoint how she felt about this new development. On the one hand she still felt that loss, that same emptiness she'd felt a half hour ago upon waking. And now, she felt disappointed and a little perturbed that he'd leave her here, alone, when her sole purpose for coming to this house this week was to be with him.

"Why do I get the distinct impression that you're not thinking of how much you'll miss him while he's away?" Beverly questioned.

Jade set her cup down, shaking her head at the same time. "Oh, I'm sorry. I was just thinking of something. Don't mind me."

With a tilt of her head Beverly looked at Jade seriously. "I don't think anyone's been minding you for some time now, Jade."

"I don't know what you mean."

"Why don't we spend the day together? The men aren't around and I'd like to get to know you better."

A sense of dread settled over Jade and she racked her brain for a logical excuse as to why that wasn't possible. Of course, with Linc gone there was none and that infuriated her even more. With a tight smile she looked at her hostess and said, "What did you have in mind?"

* * *

"So what's really going on with you and my son?"

Jade almost fell off the lounge chair she'd been lying on. Her sunglasses had fallen from the table and she'd bent over to retrieve them when Beverly's question had been asked. They'd been to the spa and had a swim. Now they were sitting poolside, enjoying the beautiful day. So far it had been pleasurable and now this.

"We're, ah…dating…I guess," she stuttered.

"Is that so?"

Repositioning herself on the chair Jade was about to slip her glasses back onto her face when Beverly touched her hand and shook her head. This, to Jade, meant that Beverly didn't want her eyes shielded because she wanted honest answers. It reminded her a lot of Grammy.

Knowing she'd have to give Mrs. Donovan a little more information and still hating the fact of all these lies building up, Jade took a deep breath and decided to tell as much of the truth as she possibly could. "We haven't seen each other in years. And when we bumped into each other last week we decided to take some time to get to know one another again."

"Hmm. I sense a connection between you two. I wonder why you stayed apart for so long."

"We were in college when we met and things just didn't seem to work out for us." Jade stared out toward the pool. "Linc had plans," she said, remembering their talk on her first day here.

Beverly chuckled. "Lincoln has had plans since he was ten years old. I always wondered if he was ever going to slow down and simply enjoy life. And I'll admit that until this week I was still thinking the same thing."

"He's a very focused man. I guess I should have realized that back then." She should have realized that he'd never be truly interested in a girl like her.

"Yes, he's ambitious. But he's also loyal and dependable. He has such a capacity to love. I just wish he'd get the chance."

Oh, no. Jade's chest tightened. She definitely did not want to be having this conversation with Linc's mother. Keeping her head turned in the opposite direction she feigned interest in some birds flying overhead. "Love is not for everyone," she said absently.

"It is if they make themselves available to it."

Jade entwined her fingers, pulled them apart then twisted them back together again. She shifted in the chair wanting desperately to get up and leave. Then she stilled, a thought settling in her mind. "Sometimes it's not that easy."

She turned when she felt the soft swish of

Beverly's silk coverlet against her leg. The older woman had come to sit on the edge of Jade's chair putting a hand over hers to stop the incessant motion. "You have to be still so it can catch you, dear," she said soothingly.

Jade turned to her then and for the first time this afternoon took a moment to really look at Mrs. Donovan. A more beautiful woman Jade couldn't remember ever seeing. But there was something more to her beauty. A calmness combined with a glow of completeness.

"If you love him, you need to tell him."

She opened her mouth to speak, fully prepared to tell the woman she didn't know what she was talking about. Her lips snapped shut and she thought better of that brazen lie. "It won't matter. It's not what he wants."

Beverly threw her head back and laughed. "Child, please. Of all my children, Lincoln, who pretends to know exactly what he wants at all times, is the most clueless. He's been so ambitious and so determined for so long he's never really had the chance to experience any true emotions. Businesses fold, money gets spent and then what's left? There's something between you two, I can sense it and I know my son. If you weren't in his heart in some capacity he would never have brought you to my home."

"But we're so different. He's from money and affluence and I'm—" Jade looked down at herself. "I'm just the daughter of a lovesick woman who couldn't bear the thought of being alone anymore and killed herself. My grandmother raised me to be proud and I am. But I also know when I'm out of my league."

Beverly waved a hand with a disdainful look on her face. "I heard about the incident with Leslie. In fact, the dimwitted girl called me herself with the sordid tale. I told her I was glad she called, but that I didn't expect to hear from her again. She's rude and ignorant and I won't tolerate that mentality." The older woman's brow furrowed as she spoke. "Bank accounts and fake levels of society, I don't give a hoot about those kinds of things. And neither do my children. They weren't raised that way. If Lincoln likes you, you can believe that your social status is the last thing on his mind."

Laying her head back against the chair Jade let out the deep breath she'd been holding in an attempt to keep her feelings at bay. "I don't know what's on Linc's mind. I'm not even sure he likes me most of the time."

Still rubbing her hands Beverly smiled reassuringly. "He likes you, dear. Believe me he likes you more than he's willing to admit."

* * *

That night when Jade was sure she'd die of loneliness she'd been treated to a surprise. She'd dressed for dinner only to learn that the older Donovans had a meeting at the club where the party was being held on Saturday night and the Donovan men, with the exception of Linc, who was still in Vegas, were out for the evening.

So she'd sat at that huge table about to consume her meal alone when she heard footsteps approaching and the distinct sound of gum cracking. That made her think of home, of…

"Hey, sis!"

"Noelle? What are you doing here?"

Noelle headed straight for her and Jade stood to greet her. Noelle hugged her tightly, which only concerned Jade more. "I asked what you're doing here?"

"Chill out, Jay. I was invited."

"Invited? By who? Nobody's here?"

Noelle took a seat and wasted no time retrieving a napkin, unfolding it and sticking it down her shirt like a bib. She reached for one of the trays in front of her and started to scoop food onto her plate.

"Noelle?" Jade yelled. "I'm talking to you."

Noelle frowned. "No. You're yelling at me because I haven't answered your questions yet.

I'm hungry. I didn't get a chance to eat today because I worked at the spa for twelve hours and then I had to run home and change and get out here." She lifted a glass and took a long gulp. "You think somebody could get me something a little stronger than wine?"

When Jade didn't answer her Noelle sighed heavily. "Sit down, Jay. You're not getting any taller."

"Don't be smart," Jade said but took her seat anyway.

"Okay, so I was working at the spa, and we were busy today. Girl, I tell you business is good. We're about to blow up!" She laughed.

We? Since when was she an active part of the spa? But that wasn't what was bothering Jade. "Do I have to ask you again?"

"No, girl. Dang, you need to loosen up. That's just what I told that fine ass Lincoln Donovan when he came waltzing into the spa this afternoon."

"What? Linc was at Happy Hands?" She gulped. "Today?"

"Mmm-hmm." Noelle chewed on a bite of salad and swallowed. "He came in and asked for me specifically. You know I tried to play like I was somebody else until he said his name and then I thought something had happened to you so I was about to jack him up."

Jade dropped her head into her hands. "Noelle, please tell me you didn't strike the man."

"No, but he was damn close to it, especially since you weren't with him and he was being real secretive about his reason for being there. But anyway, he looked around for a bit then he made a call on his cell. Then when I thought he was about to leave he came over and told me he knew about the money. Now, Jay, if you were gonna tell him it was my debt then why didn't you just let me handle it from the get-go?"

"I don't want to talk about your debt right now, Noelle." And she didn't. Her head was pounding and questions still bubbled around in her mind. Why had Linc gone to her shop? And why had he sent Noelle out here?

"Whatever. So he says that you might need some company tonight since he had some business to tend to so he sent me a car when the spa closed and had me brought out here. And from the looks of it—" Noelle looked along the span of the empty dining room table "—he wasn't lying."

Jade sat back in her chair. So he'd known she would be alone tonight. And he'd thought to send her sister to keep her company. She wasn't sure if she was touched or outraged. An evening with Noelle was not entertainment, it was slow torture.

But she had missed seeing her sister so she wouldn't give the angry thoughts too much time. "So you said the spa's doing well? How many new clients did we get this week? Or were they just returns?"

"Oh, no, those coupons you gave out at the convention last weekend were coming in left and right. And the referral slips from that slinky hotel, they're working out, too. I'd say about five new clients and at least a dozen tourists have been in so far. Kent says it's a step in the right direction."

"It certainly sounds like it."

"Mmm-hmm," Noelle nodded then finished off her salad.

Jade continued to think over the numbers she'd just heard and ways to keep this good streak going. She'd almost forgotten Noelle was even there when her sister poked the back of her hand with a fork. "Ow! What'd you do that for?"

"Because I asked you a question."

"Oh, no, you're not getting all feisty because I didn't give you a quick answer when I just had to wait twenty minutes to get one measly answer out of you."

"At least I heard your question. You aren't even listening to me."

Because she was right Jade backed down. "I'm sorry. What were you saying?"

"I said, what's going on with you and Lincoln? He looked like Sad Dog Sam and you're looking a little on the slumpy side yourself. So I'm wondering what you two have been up to these past few days."

If Jade had heard this question a moment ago she certainly would have ignored it. Now, it seemed she didn't have a choice but to provide some sort of answer. "Nothing's going on."

"You lie and you don't do it well. Try again," Noelle said smartly.

Jade frowned. "Okay, I slept with him. Is that what you wanted to hear?"

"No," Noelle said smiling. "But it's a start."

"It's not a start. Linc and I never had a start. It always seems as if we're ending," she said quietly.

"What's that supposed to mean? You're back together aren't you?"

"I told you the other night we weren't together. This is just a job for the week to get the debt erased. Sunday morning I'll be packing my bags and heading home to my real life."

"And Linc will be where?"

"He'll be here and then he'll be at his hotel or wherever. He just won't be with me." To her ears that sounded pitiful and desolate. So much so she wanted to cry.

"Now were those his words or are you improvising?"

"I don't improvise, Noelle."

Noelle nodded in agreement. "No, you don't. But you do overreact. So did he say he didn't want to see you again after Sunday? I mean, did he specifically tell you that he wanted you to be gone for good?"

Jade rubbed her hands over her face. She did not want to be having this conversation with her younger sister. Noelle had never had anything but good luck with men. How could she ever understand what Jade was going through? "No. He didn't say those words exactly. But I know what the deal is. I'm not stupid."

Noelle pulled a cigarette out of her bag and prepared to light up.

"Don't do that in here," Jade screeched and grabbed the cigarette from her sister's hand. "You need to quit this nasty habit anyway."

"I need to do a lot of things but right now we're working on you and your needs. Now either show me to the porch or the deck, or since they're rich, the smoking room, because I can't wait another minute."

Jade stood and they walked through the patio door out into the cool night air. Jade inhaled deeply as she took a seat in one of the chairs at the glass-top table. Noelle instantly lit up and took a long puff.

Blowing smoke into the air she turned to Jade and asked, "So you slept with him and now you're the one doing the leaving?"

Jade's head snapped in her direction. "Don't even put me in the same category as him."

"It's all good. Maybe you think it's your turn to get a little revenge. I can certainly understand that after all that crying you did over him."

Jade did not cry over Linc, at least not for that long. And she'd already sought her revenge, a fact which was also causing her great distress. "Having sex with Linc and leaving him was never my plan. Having sex with him wasn't my plan."

"But you did it anyway. Why?"

"Because I couldn't help myself." Then Jade sighed and decided to be real and honest with herself and her sister. "Because I can't stop loving him."

That shut Noelle right up.

For about ten seconds.

"Then you need to stop trippin' and get your man."

"It's not that simple, Noelle." This was the second time in one day that another woman had told her what she needed to do where Linc was concerned. But Jade had never gone to Noelle about matters of the heart. Her sister had a slightly different idea about relationships and love than Jade did. In short, Noelle didn't believe in love. She did, however, believe in sexing yourself crazy, so knowing that Jade had always said Linc was the best in bed she'd ever had sort of contributed to Noelle's rooting for him.

"It's a simple as you want it to be. Or, in your case, as hard as you make it." She stamped out her cigarette in the ash tray and scooted her chair closer to Jade's. Taking her sister's hand she looked her right in the face. "You've been the big sister. You've been the granddaughter. You're the boss at Happy Hands and you're the best person I know. You deserve some happiness. So if Linc makes you happy I say go for it."

"But we don't want the same things."

"How do you know? Did you ask him what he wanted? Better yet, did you tell him what you wanted?"

Jade sighed. She hadn't told him. Yesterday, she'd given him stipulations and when he blamed those stipulations on her residual feelings from her breakup with Charles she'd let him go on thinking that was the cause. She hadn't told him that she was crying for the love he'd never known she had for him. Or for the relationship that could never be because he wasn't that type of man.

"What's the point? He told me that the reason he left me eight years ago was because he knew that I was a forever kind of girl and that he couldn't do forever."

"Jay, that was eight damn years ago. How do you know what he's willing to do now? And does it have to be all or nothing right at this moment? Damn, does he have to propose to you right now for you to believe he's worthy?"

Jade's answer was simple. "Yes. He either loves me or he doesn't. There's no middle ground with Linc and I. There can't be. I can't take it."

She'd begun to cry and instead of Noelle continuing with her comments she, for the first time in their lives, held and consoled her big sister.

Friday was the tour arranged by Beverly. Jade had to give it to the woman, she sure knew how to celebrate in style.

Linc returned during breakfast, at which time Jade did not question why he'd left. It didn't matter anymore. She'd emptied her soul to Noelle last night. And when Noelle had gone home she'd lain in their room, alone, thinking about Beverly's advice. Maybe she should just tell Linc how she felt. Maybe their social status didn't matter. And maybe, just maybe, he did have more feelings for her than she knew.

Even if luck were on her side and all of the above were true there was still one huge obstacle standing in their way—she'd stolen from him.

She'd considered telling him at least a dozen times since they'd made love. But then her feelings had resurfaced and she'd been so preoccupied with her self-preservation she didn't think of it. That was understandable considering the odds of a woman falling in love with the same man twice were slim to none.

Guilt was a steady companion for Jade these days. In her defense, things were different between her and Linc when she'd decided to do what she did. She was angry about his proposition and even angrier about the fact that she had no choice but to go along with it. And now she was stuck in a web of deceit with a man she'd loved all of her adult life. What was she going to do?

She'd have to figure that out later. Today, they were going on a mini cruise to tour the Hoover Dam. Then they were heading to the Grand Canyon in a fleet of rented Hummers courtesy of the Donovans. About twenty of them were going on the little excursion, so she didn't have the worry of being alone with Linc and thus wouldn't have to deal with the growing conflict between them.

Jade was headed down the steps when Trent joined her.

"All set to go?" he asked.

"Yup. And you?"

"To tell the truth I'm ready for this week to be over. Mom's running us ragged with all these activities."

They walked together down the rest of the steps with Jade feeling as if this was her home, that she really belonged here. That was a dangerous feeling she knew and struggled to check it quickly. "I've enjoyed it. It's not going to be easy returning to my solitary life."

"I thought you had a sister."

"I do. But she has her own life. I'm a solo adult now." She shrugged trying to brush off the sudden wave of pity she felt for herself.

Trent stopped and looked directly at her. "Not anymore."

"What?"

"You have Linc now."

Trent looked at her as if he knew what her response to that would be. That was weird, and she paused to examine him a moment. "I don't have Linc. We're dating and that's all." That wasn't totally a lie but still she berated herself. In this past week she'd become a liar and a thief, the two most hated people in her world.

"You don't think that'll turn into something more?"

She smiled and laid a hand on Trent's shoulder. "Whatever happens between Linc and I is our business."

"I second that," Linc spoke, appearing mysteriously in the doorway.

Leaning against the doorjamb, a beige T-shirt molding against his well-defined chest, slacks buttoned at his narrow waist, and even though his eyes flashed with a touch of temper, he looked magnificent. She watched him approach feeling her lungs constrict with each step he took wondering what it would really feel like to be in a relationship with him. But that was a foolish thought. Not only did he not want a relationship, once he found out she'd stolen from him he might follow through with his earlier threat and have her arrested.

"That it is," Trent said to his brother. "We shall all find out sooner or later."

Jade suspected that Trent was now baiting Linc the way he'd just attempted to do her. She liked Trent. He was certainly easy enough to look at but he questioned everything relentlessly. She wondered if he ever stopped asking questions long enough to find his own woman.

Linc nodded then took Jade's hand and headed toward the door. "Maybe so but right now we're on our way to learn more about the Hoover Dam."

Jade marveled at the sights she'd seen today. The ride on the Desert Princess had been fun. She and Linc had stood side by side along the deck of the Mississippi-style paddle wheeler as it puttered along Lake Mead which she'd learned was the world's largest man-made lake. And for two hours they'd visited the Dam.

Linc apparently had taken this tour before as he was her designated guide for the day, reciting historical facts, pointing out the best views and holding her hand. Now while your normal tour guide certainly didn't go to this extreme, Jade felt very good that he did.

By late afternoon they were boarding the luxury SUVs, which by the way were the ugliest vehicles she had ever seen. Of course, the men were enamored, each one vowing to look into purchasing one as soon as he returned home.

She watched with a swelling heart the way the Donovan brothers interacted. They were without a doubt very close. The Triple Threat Brothers, that's exactly what they were. A triple dose of good looks, brains and money designed to break the hearts of millions of women.

A moment of foreboding had Jade finally accepting the fact that she was number one million and one.

On the ride to the Grand Canyon she was silent, wrapped in thoughts of her latest mistake. Why had she thought she could spend an entire week with Linc and escape unscathed? The answer to that question was irrelevant as her only goal now was to make it through tonight and tomorrow without foolishly revealing her feelings to him. No good could come from telling Linc that she'd fallen in love with him all over again.

He traced a finger along her cheek while leaning close to her ear. "What's on your mind?"

She didn't pull away, didn't try to resist his touch. She was too far gone for that. "Nothing, really."

"You look worried."

She tried valiantly for a smile. "What could I possibly have to worry about?" A mere glance in his eyes gave her heart a flutter and she had the answer to her question. He was looking at her as if there were no greater view. When he found out she'd stolen from him and fallen in love with him all in the span of a week, that look would turn to pure disgust. And that, she knew, would break her heart more completely than any man ever had.

"Come on, the sun's about to set. We don't want to miss this view."

The vehicle had stopped but she hadn't noticed. Placing her hand in his she let him lead her out toward the end of the cliff they'd parked on.

The sky was now a fierce compilation of orange and gold, layers upon layers of intense color blending together to frame the sun's magnificent descent. Sharp peaks of burnt-orange rock jutted upward giving rise to smooth centers and what looked to be a carefully sculpted masterpiece.

Jade was overwhelmed by nature's performance. "It's beautiful," she whispered.

Linc, who had his arm securely around her waist, turned her to face him at that moment. "Yes. It is."

Her throat constricted as his eyes focused solely on her. He had her in a full embrace now, her breasts pressed firmly against his chest.

"There is nothing else like it in the world," he whispered, lowering his head dangerously close to hers. "You are perfect."

She thought it was the altitude that stole her breath, but something told her it was simply the man. "Linc," she whispered when his lips were so close she could almost taste him.

"Ask me, Jade. Ask me to kiss you."

Oh, God, she wanted to. Every nerve in her body stood on end those moments he hovered close to her and she wanted nothing more than to pucker up and accept what he was so graciously offering. But that wouldn't be enough. She needed much more than he was willing to give.

She turned away. "I can't." He still held her and that, too, was a mistake. She backed away from him.

"I'm not what you think I am and I can't do this with you anymore." She needed to tell him about the supplies she'd purchased on his credit card. She needed to tell him that she'd repay that amount even though she had no idea how or when. Most importantly she needed to tell him this charade was over and that as soon as she got back to the Donovan estate she was going to pack her bags and head home to Vegas.

"I don't think either one of us can deny whatever this is between us anymore, Jade."

He hadn't moved from where he stood and although her back was to him she could almost see the tortured expression on his face. "There is nothing between us. Nothing but this ridiculous agreement we came up with." *And the thousands of dollars I now owe you.*

He grabbed her by her shoulders spinning her around to face him. "You can't run away from it."

"Me? Running? No, Linc, that's your department. What I'm doing is being realistic. I don't want to make love with you for the rest of the week and then go on about my business."

"Stop throwing that up in my face," he growled as he gave her shoulders a little shake. "I know I left and I know I was wrong. I've apologized for that. The mere fact that you're here means that you've either forgiven the mistake or at least forgotten it. So don't bring it up again."

"You can't boss me around! I'm not one of your employees." The minute the words were out she knew what his response would be.

"You are, in fact, my employee. But that's not what this is about," he said quietly.

"It's not?" She dared to hope.

He let out a deep breath, looking as frustrated as she felt. "Look, we need to talk and we can't do it here. Let's just enjoy the view and we'll deal with the other stuff later."

She nodded her agreement knowing instinctively that when they did talk later she wasn't going to feel much better about things than she did now.

Linc wasted no time excusing them from drinks after dinner. Since their encounter on the cliff he'd thought of nothing but being alone with her. He'd tried to play by her rules, tried to keep from taking her the way he wanted to, the way he knew she wanted him to. But today had just been too much.

She'd looked stunning in all white, her hair tucked back behind her ears, her eyes sparkling with each new sight he'd shown her. She'd laughed, she'd listened, she'd simply been and he wanted her, completely.

She wanted him too. A man could tell these things and he knew without a doubt that she was fighting it but couldn't understand why. That was all well and good. Tonight she would lose the battle.

Once in their suite Jade slipped off her shoes and fell back on the bed. She was exhausted, every inch of her body hurt and she longed for a nice hot bath and some sleep. She heard his voice and knew instinctively that she would not be getting either anytime soon.

"Let me help you," he said as he lifted a foot and began to massage. "You know you're not the only one who can give a massage."

He was correct. His fingers were working some mean magic on her feet, sending twinges up and down her legs. Tilting her head back she marveled in the feeling. "Mmm. You keep this up and I might offer you a job."

He chuckled. "No thanks. I reserve this treatment for special people."

Her head snapped up and she glared at him. "Am I to assume I'm special?"

Linc looked at her seriously. "There's no assumption to be made. You are very special to me, Jade." Letting her foot slip back to the floor he slid his hands up her leg to rest on her thigh.

She shook her head. "Lincoln, don't." She couldn't take another minute of his sweetness. He'd driven her mad with it all day and if he continued she didn't know that she'd have the strength to stop him and she so desperately needed to stop him.

With his free hand he brought a finger to her lips. "Shh. I don't want you to say another word." His gaze fell to her mouth as his finger moved slowly over her bottom lip. "It's been an extremely long day."

She gasped, her lips parting slowly. He slipped his finger inside and she impulsively sucked.

He closed his eyes, let out a whoosh of air then said, "A really long day."

She moved back, dislodging his finger from her mouth. "Yes," she whispered.

"I want you to relax." He spoke quietly, his

hand now cupping her cheek. "I'm going to take good care of you. Trust me."

She trusted that with each touch from him her body temperature would continue to rise. She also trusted that she had the option to make an informed choice when or if the time arose. He pushed her back on the bed, settling her on the pillows. They hadn't turned on the lights when they'd come in so they were illuminated only by slivers of moonlight coming through the partially opened drapes.

"I'm going to touch you, Jade." He began by unbuttoning her pants, pulling them along with her panties down her legs. "I'm going to touch you a lot."

His gaze, bold and filled with desire raked over her continuously. She sucked in a breath, felt the twinges of nervousness snaking up her spine. Cool air hit her legs and before she could speak he was working her blouse over her head. She now lay totally nude before him and while she was in no way ashamed of her body she was a little uncomfortable with the way he stared down at her.

"I told you. Perfect." He sighed then ran a fingertip around the darkened area of her breast.

He circled and circled until her nipple hardened sharply. Bending down he ran his tongue over the distended crest and felt her tremble beneath him.

Pulling away he repeated the combination with the other breast all the while keeping an eye on her, watching her every reaction.

His finger made a scorching line down her torso stopping at her navel, where he bent and showered her with tongue attention. She shifted slightly and he smiled against her.

Desire ran through her with an urgency that threatened to shatter her. Never had she felt so wanted, so cherished. Never had she needed so honestly, so completely. He touched her gently yet she knew he was using every ounce of control he possessed to do so. He'd told her to trust him and she'd decided to do just that. Wherever he was taking them, tonight and just for tonight, she'd go. And go willingly.

Linc's touch was masterful, caressing then gripping with the urgency he contained. He was greedy and hungry, this she knew, yet he was restraining his own needs to cater to hers, to take what she silently offered.

Jade simply flowed with him, with his touch, his caresses. He'd instructed her to relax but then he continued to touch her until she was taut with need. He was massaging her thighs now, his thumbs just tickling the insides, barely missing the nest of dark curls at her center. Her breathing stalled then restarted as he pushed her thighs apart, traced a finger lazily down the center of her opening.

"Linc," she whispered.

"Let me love you, baby," he spoke just before lowering his head.

Jade spread her legs wider, gripped the back of his head and blessedly acquiesced. His tongue moved slowly, sinuously, from her top to her bottom, soliciting from her deep moans of satisfaction. With his thumbs he spread her lips then flattened his tongue and lathed her thoroughly.

She squirmed and bucked, gripping the sheets beneath her to keep from screaming. If she died this very moment she'd go happily. Sensations twirled through her while her essence seeped out. With the pad of his thumb pressed lightly against the bud of her flower Linc proceeded to work his magnificent tongue over her opening until she thought she just simply couldn't take it another moment.

"Linc, please?" she whimpered.

She wanted this man, all of him, in any way she could have him. If it were just for tonight then so be it, she'd deal with her broken heart next week. But for right now, for this one moment she wanted, no, needed him deeply inside of her and if that wasn't an informative decision then brand her a fool. But by the end of tonight she'd be a well-satisfied fool.

Chapter 11

Linc accepted her agreement in the way her hands gripped his head tightly, the way her thighs clenched and retracted with his ministrations and the way she fed him like a wanton sure of her power. He acknowledged her participation and thanked her lavishly with each stroke and lick.

She dulled his senses, captured him so completely like no other woman had ever done before. Moving his lips over her soft flesh he relished in each of her convulsions. She held his head firmly daring him to move and he smiled inwardly. He had her just where he wanted her.

* * *

Jade closed her eyes not realizing that made the sensations all the more potent and soul shattering. What was he doing to her? It wasn't simply pleasure. No, this was well beyond that. She practically floated, dangled helplessly as he manipulated her. That, she realized the moment she felt herself slipping closer to the edge, was his intention. He wanted her helpless, defenseless to his onslaught. He wanted to control her.

She wanted to protest but he continued to suck, to lap, to lick, to stroke her into submission, in that mindless swirl of contentment she hadn't known existed until now. Her head thrashed about the pillows as she rose toward the precipice of completion.

Linc felt her soaring—she knew it because he lifted her hips, propped her up so that he had more access, more control over this sweet torture he'd instigated. He devoured her, feasting on her offering as if he'd been unjustly starved.

She moaned. It didn't seem to be enough. She sighed and panted. Still the release did not come. "Linc," she whimpered his name. He thrust his hot tongue inside of her and she fell.

Down that dark bottomless spiral that had sucked her in from the moment he'd first laid his hands on her. Falling and falling, that sense of weightlessness and completion that engulfed you body and soul. She called his name until her lips wouldn't move any longer. Then and only then did he release his hold on her to slide sinuously up her body.

"Ask me to kiss you, Jade," he demanded.

She heard his voice, heard his command and knew her response even before her lips parted. "Kiss me, Linc."

The night began and ended with his mouth on her, first at her center and then on her lips. But that was as far as he went.

To her surprise Linc hadn't entered her. He hadn't found his own pleasure. He hadn't even tried.

Still, Jade lay naked, sated and completely exhausted, her head nestled in the crook of Linc's arm. She sighed and he shifted.

"You finally awake, sleepyhead?" He kissed the top of her head.

"Mmm. Yes, I'm awake."

"Good, because I didn't want to be accused of leaving you again but I do have some business to tend to."

She shifted and propped herself up on her elbow. "Is it the same business that took you back to Vegas?"

"Yes." He looked as if he wanted to say something else but refrained.

"You could have gone. I would have understood," she said sincerely. She understood a lot about Lincoln Donovan now.

He rubbed a hand up and down her back. "The truth is I wasn't ready to leave you just yet."

"Oh?" They were silent for a moment and then she remembered something she'd meant to do yesterday. "Thank you."

He looked at her questioningly. "For?"

"For sending my sister to keep me company. I really needed that. And it was very thoughtful of you to do it."

"I knew you needed something. I figured since it wasn't me, it would definitely be her. And it gave me a chance to meet her."

"So what did you think?"

Linc chuckled. "I think you two are as different as night and day. I also think she loves you very much and that she'll be just fine when you cut the apron strings."

"Just how long did you two talk and what exactly did you talk about?"

"That's between Noelle and me. I'll just say that we now have an understanding about her gambling habits."

"I sure do hope so. I can't afford to make these types of deals with every casino owner in Vegas."

"You'd better not make these types of deals with every casino owner in Vegas," Linc warned.

She laughed then. A happy laugh that she wasn't sure she'd be able to share with him again.

He kissed her forehead and then moved to her lips. "I'm not laughing, Jade."

And after another moment, neither was she.

Hours later, Linc sat on the couch in the suite, a pile of mail right beside him. Jade watched him methodically go through one piece at a time. She'd finished dressing and wanted to go riding one last time.

She'd be leaving the Donovan estate first thing tomorrow morning. Noelle would no longer owe him five thousand dollars. Those were the terms of their agreement and she planned to abide by them.

But she didn't want to think of that right now.

Right now she was content with the memories of last night, of Linc's tenderness. He'd held her close, loved her just right and kissed her with the sweetness of a man who cared about a woman.

"How long is that going to take?" she asked, nodding toward the stack of mail.

"About an hour," he said glancing up at her. "If I go through it all."

She smiled, happy for this time alone with him. "And are you going through it all?"

He shook his head. "Not if you have something more appealing for me to do."

"How about riding?"

He stood then moved toward her. Slipping his arms around her waist he pulled her close. "I want to be wherever you are," he said, dropping a kiss on her neck then nuzzling.

Jade relished this feeling. "I'll take that as a yes."

"So you still don't know anything about her past?"

"For Pete's sake, Trent. Give it a rest," Adam bellowed.

Linc sighed. "For once I agree with Adam."

Trent moved to the bar to fix himself a drink. "She's got the both of you snowed. My gut instinct says she's hiding something."

"That's gas," Adam quipped.

Trent tossed him an impatient glance. "That's five years of Navy Seal duties, investigating the enemy."

"She's not a spy or a traitor for that matter," Linc offered.

He and Jade had returned from their ride about an hour ago and she was now getting some much needed rest. Looking around the den he could have kicked himself for not joining her.

"No. She's an attractive woman who's gotten under your skin."

"Has she really?" Adam's eyes shifted to Linc. "Has my big brother fallen in love?"

Linc ignored them both.

The look Trent gave him said that wasn't the response he was looking for.

"She's a wonderful woman. A man would be hard-pressed to find better," he stated seriously.

"If it's getting serious maybe you should check her out, Linc," Adam added.

Linc shot him a testy glare. "I thought you were on my side."

"I am, but we all know how women are, especially with guys like us. Hell, you're the one who educated me."

Linc ran a hand over his face. Upstairs on his desk was an envelope. In it was something he hoped would put him and Jade on an even keel. That was all he was concerning himself with tonight. His brothers' words were not fazing him at all.

Jade stepped out of the limousine in front of Chase Country Club, a gorgeous structure complete with gleaming white pillars and floor-to-ceiling windows. Twinkle lights illuminated the outside walkway giving the distinctive feeling of Christmas in the summertime. She inhaled deeply and willed the butterflies that seemed to have taken up permanent residence in her stomach to cease. She wasn't nervous, she told herself repeatedly. There was no need to be. She'd been with Linc all week long and with his family. Truth be told she felt like she belonged with them more than she did in her tiny apartment.

But this was her last night. She felt like Cinderella when she glanced down at her watch. She was right on time. Linc and his brothers had come earlier to make sure that everything was in place since this was the one event Beverly hadn't planned herself. In a little over eleven hours she'd be on her way back to Vegas, back to the life she believed she wanted for herself.

That hadn't really changed much. Her spa was still a top priority. It was the other, the happily ever after, that she'd be pushing aside yet again. At least this time it was of her own doing. She decided the outcome to this episode. She wanted a man to love her and Linc was incapable of that. Case closed.

Although thoughts of her and Linc building a life together had run rampant through her mind since waking up this morning, she was determined not to let them interfere. A one-sided relationship was doomed to fail. Besides, the last thing in the world he'd want is to be with her after he found out what she'd done. She'd decided earlier that she had to tell him tonight. She owed him that much and her conscience would never leave her alone if she didn't.

A bellboy dressed in a crisp white uniform opened the door for her and directed her to the lobby. Walking confidently in three-inch heels Jade stopped when she stood in the middle of a champagne-colored marble floor, stark white pillars stretching from ceiling to floor in regal elegance as tropical plants littered the room. The concierge questioned where she was headed before smiling and pointing her toward the ballroom.

Her heels clicked against the polished floors as she made her way to the entrance of the infamous ballroom. Candles burned and chandeliers above lit the room so that it sparkled with elegant festivity. Waiters in black slacks and white jackets moved from table to table making sure everything was set perfectly while kitchen staff carefully organized the table of hors d'oeuvres amidst a giant ice sculpture in the shape of two Mustangs. Jade smiled as she remembered the Donovans' fondness of horses.

She would miss them, she thought sadly.

Beverly had been the mother figure Jade had always longed for, while Henry, in his carefree manner, had welcomed her with open arms. Her chest tightened and she willed herself not to cry. It wasn't meant to be. She'd known that this was just a job and that it was only supposed to last a week. She should have been prepared for the end.

But she wasn't and the end was inevitable.

That's how Linc found her. Her lithe frame draped in a shimmering silver material that molded against the curving contours of her body, standing on heels that were surely designed to torture a man. His eyes slowly drifted from the hem of the shining material up the enticing path of her small ankles to shapely calves and a shocking amount of muscled thigh. His breath hitched and he moved instinctively toward her.

Her thick ebony hair was pulled away from her face in a sweep of curls that cascaded down her otherwise bare back. The dress dipped dangerously low in the back, so low that the shadow of her hair cleverly masked the initial indentation of her bottom. Linc licked his suddenly dry lips and searched for a waiter to bring him a drink. She moved, angling her head to study something on the ice sculpture. The curve of her neck was exposed and smooth skin glistened beneath the many lights. All the blood drained from his head, quickly moving south, as he clearly remembered dragging his tongue slowly down the long angle beginning at the tips of her tiny ears and ending with lavish circles around her bare shoulder. His hands fisted and clenched at his sides as he noticed other men in the room admiring her.

It was inevitable that she'd be admired. She was beautiful. But she was his. His? He'd been considering all day what that meant since the thought had cemented itself in his mind. She was supposed to leave tomorrow morning but he had no intention of letting that happen.

Coming up behind her he bent his head until his nose was tickled by wisps of her hair. He inhaled deeply the sweet smell of lavender invading his senses inciting prickly spikes at the base of his neck. Like a moth to a flame his finger found that small spot just beneath her ear, the one that had caught his attention from across the room, and traced a long, slow line down her neck, ending on her shoulder where it made delicate circles over the soft skin.

Jade hissed. She'd felt his approach, heat rising from the center of her belly to her now throbbing breasts. She'd anticipated his touch, longed for it, embraced it. He was hers. In her mind he would always be hers.

She turned to face him, became enfolded in his

embrace and looked up into his eyes. Those dark eyes that held all his secrets. She'd watched them change and shift with his moods, deciding finally that she liked them all because they made him the man that he was. The man she loved.

But he didn't love her. No. She slapped that thought aside. She would not think of that now, not tonight. His strong jaw was set and his lips parted slightly. Dressed in a tuxedo he looked dark, dangerous and oh, so delicious! "Mr. Donovan, I'm reporting for duty," she said a bit too airily.

As it was whenever he was close to her his senses dulled, his mind emptying of all sane thought. She had applied makeup tonight; vibrant slashes of blue and silver glittered over her eyes making them dance and sparkle in the lighted room, enhancing her natural beauty. Her nose was narrow with a sharp tip but her mouth looked soft coated with a light lipstick and damned kissable right at this moment.

"You're punctual. I like that." His voice was deep but gentle as his eyes held hers. Something powerful slammed into his gut, an emotion he couldn't describe.

"That's just one of my traits worth boasting. Now, what would you like me to do?" To her own ears the question sounded way too suggestive. She hoped he'd heard it differently.

His eyes darkened, his lids closing so that they were barely visible, and he moved closer to her so that the tips of her breasts brushed against his solid chest. Obviously, he'd heard her and deciphered the meaning.

"I mean, I'm not real clear on my job duties tonight. Should I just stay by your side?" To keep herself upright she flattened her hands against the lapels of his jacket. The walls seemed to close in around them and she felt as if she were suffocating.

"It's simple." His hands slipped inside the opening at her back. "You stay right beside me looking absolutely scrumptious. Which, by the way, you do very well. We'll have dinner, dance a little and then at the stroke of midnight run like bats out of hell to the car where Mario has already been instructed to burn rubber getting us home."

He made it sound so simple, she thought. Like standing beside him wasn't going to be hard enough. She had to smile and be cordial, too, as if her body weren't raging with desire, and then she had the thought of what would happen once they got home. Home, she thought wistfully. But it wasn't her home. *Hush!* she yelled to that pesky inner voice. Tonight it would be.

"That sounds like a plan," she said.

Her smile was dazzling, her body soft and pliant in his arms. Man, he wanted her so badly he could already taste her essence on his tongue. His groin tensed at the thought and she looked at him questioningly. "It's your fault. You're a minx and you've got me under your spell."

Jade continued to smile. If he were under her spell then she might as well take complete advantage of him. "That's right, so I don't expect you to go wandering off with any other female. Tonight—" she stood on tiptoe and nipped his bottom lip "—you belong to me."

About an hour into the evening, after Jade had been introduced to the fifty or so people she hadn't already met, they had dinner. A delicious meal that she knew she most likely would not be having again in the near future. She'd sat at the head table with the family, Linc on one side of her and Adam on the other.

The music started shortly after dessert was served and with Linc's strained approval she danced with Adam and Trent again. His cousins had women fawning over them and didn't pay her a bit of attention, which she was sure Linc didn't mind. What was funny was the look on his face each time she passed him on the dance floor. Of course, since she'd been dancing with someone else a female was bound to come by and scoop him up. He looked as if he'd died and gone straight to hell!

She and Adam had a ball laughing over that. Finally, she'd gone to rescue him, tapping a very attractive young woman on the shoulder and asking to interrupt. Of course the woman looked at her as if she had two heads but Jade didn't care—Linc was already releasing her and pulling Jade securely in his arms.

"What took you so long? I've been waiting for you to rescue me for more than fifteen minutes."

He was so handsome and so oblivious to the fact that he was selling himself short by not allowing himself to fall in love. "I could have saved you eight years ago," she said without another thought.

"We weren't the same people eight years ago," he said after staring at her a few seconds.

"This is true," she conceded not wanting the mistakes of their past to intrude on this perfect moment of the present.

"So what will you do with yourself now that Noelle isn't going to need you so much?" he asked as they continued to glide with the music.

Tilting her head to the side she gave him a quick smile. "How do you know she's not going to need me?"

"Because she has a full-time job now."

"Really?"

"Since she loves to be in the casinos I figured I'd give her a job in mine. That way I can keep an eye on her."

Jade thought for a moment. "Why would you do that?"

"Because it's about time somebody else did it besides you. Not that I think she'll need it. Noelle's a lot smarter than I think you give her credit for."

"I never doubted she was smart. She just doesn't make smart decisions."

"Well, I think that'll be changing in the future. So you'll have more time to concentrate on other things."

"I guess you're right." She let her head rest on his shoulder and for a second simply enjoyed him. He'd done a lot of nice things for her this week, things she could let convince her that he had feelings for her. Luckily she knew better. "What will you do with yourself when I'm gone? Lock yourself back in your office?"

He stared down at her with an expression she couldn't identify then without another word he pulled her out to the pool area.

"About tomorrow," he began when they were standing alone away from the noise of the ballroom. "I have another proposition for you,"

She raised a brow. "A proposition?"

"Yes, I—"

"He needs to be excused for just a second," Trent said, grabbing hold of Linc's arm.

Both Linc and Jade looked at him wondering where he'd come from.

"What are you doing? I'm trying to talk to Jade. *Alone,*" Linc reiterated.

"I know but you need to come with us first." Trent looked to Adam for support.

"He's right, Linc, you should come with us."

To Jade Adam's voice sounded a little stony but he continued to stare at his brother and not at her.

"Its fine," she said because she felt an urgency from both the Donovans and she had a feeling that she wasn't going to like Linc's proposition. "I need to go to the ladies' room, so you guys can talk while I'm gone."

She turned to walk away and Linc grabbed her arm. "Hurry back," he said softly.

She nodded. "I will."

"You'd better have a damned good reason for interrupting," Linc exploded the minute Jade was out of earshot.

Trent ignored the remark. "Did you know she was engaged?"

Linc didn't answer.

"Six months ago, Linc. She was engaged to a

man named Charles Benson and then the wedding mysteriously never took place."

"I knew that," Linc said tightly then turned his back to his brothers. "Is this what you rushed out here to tell me?"

"No, we came to tell you that she needs money and she needs it like yesterday. Apparently her sister has a knack for getting into trouble," Adam added. "Linc, are you listening? She's trying to get to you so you can pay off her debts."

"Which one of you went behind my back and had her checked out?" he asked solemnly.

"I did," Trent admitted. "And it was a good thing. She's already stolen your credit card and run up a sizable amount."

Linc shook his head. He'd read the report late this afternoon. Everything they were telling him he already knew. "I told you I would handle it, Trent."

"How? By falling in love with her? I saw this coming and that's why I had her investigated. She's just like the rest of them, Linc. She's the reason we've all decided never to marry."

"She's not like that," Linc insisted even though his brother's words pricked dangerously close to the surface.

"I didn't think she was, either," Adam began. "But let's be realistic. Why else would she agree to come here and spend the week with you? You said yourself you haven't seen her in eight years. And I'm sure that was your choice."

Linc couldn't stand it anymore. His mind was whirling with thoughts and opinions and his usually cool, in-charge demeanor was starting to crumble. "I paid her all right!" he yelled, turning away from his brothers again.

For a few minutes there was silence, nothing but the breeze whispering over the lighted pool water.

Then they were by his side, each with questions in his eyes.

"You paid her?" Trent asked.

"Are you crazy? Because I know you're not desperate," Adam said incredulously.

Running a hand down his face, Linc took a deep breath. "No. I'm not crazy or desperate." He looked at his brothers, the two closest people to him, the two he trusted more than anyone in this world and decided it was time to come clean. "You were right about her sister. She lost some money in my casino and Jade came to work out terms to pay the money back but she didn't have the cash. I proposed she spend the week with me instead." In truth he'd offered her the way out because he wanted another night with her. Eight years ago she'd pierced his heart and he'd never admitted it to anyone, not even himself. But the moment he saw her he knew he had to have her again.

It only took him a week to realize that he wanted more than that.

"So not only is she stealing money from you, but she owes you money, too? Linc, what are you doing?" Trent argued.

"I know what I'm doing."

"Do you?" Adam asked. "I mean, you're the big brother. You're the one always in control, always with the answers. But I've got to tell you, right now I'm not sure you're headed in the right direction. This woman is out to trap you."

"She can't trap me as long as she owes me," Linc said quietly.

"What does that mean?"

"It means that I was going to offer her another job, not offer to marry her."

Two pair of eyes stared at him in question and the plan that he'd only thought about all day long was about to be revealed. Only it was supposed to be revealed to Jade first. "I'm getting an apartment for both of us and as long as she stays she doesn't have to be responsible for anything financially."

"What?" the younger Donovan brothers asked simultaneously.

* * *

Jade hadn't really gone to the ladies' room but she had crossed the length of the room twice hoping that gave the brothers enough time to talk. She'd asked Linc about his plans once she was gone and he'd been about to tell her. Why he needed privacy for that she wasn't sure. The only reason one wanted privacy was to say something important. No, she shook her head vehemently, Linc definitely did not want privacy for that. He hadn't even come close to telling her he loved her let alone proposing to her.

It had to be something else. But what? His brothers had interrupted and once again she'd felt as if she were the odd man out, or woman as it were. They talked around her as if she weren't there. Which was weird in and of itself because they'd all just shared dinner together and had talked amiably. In fact, she and Adam had formed a pretty cool relationship in her book. So why all the secrecy now? And why the stilted looks?

She'd had enough of wondering. She was going back to find out what the hell was going on. And if they didn't tell her, that was fine, but at least leave her and Linc alone to finish their business. She'd decided that she was going to tell him about the money tonight, before they left the party. If she were going to spend one last night in his arms, she wanted it to be with total honesty between them. No more secrets.

She approached the pool house and slipped through the slight opening in the door that she'd left previously. They were standing closer to the pool now, the younger Donovans surrounding Linc. They could pass for triplets, she thought whimsically. Each of them, tall, dark and extremely handsome. Each of them successful in their own rights. Each of them scared to death of committing to a woman. What a shame, she thought shaking her head and moving forward.

"She can't trap me as long as she owes me," Linc said quietly.

"What does that mean?" Adam asked.

"It means that I was going to offer her another job, not offer to marry her. I'm getting an apartment for both of us and as long as she stays she doesn't have to be responsible for anything financially."

"What?" Before she'd given it any thought her mouth had opened and she'd spoken. Now all three of them turned to her. Slowly, she walked toward them.

"Jade—" Linc began moving toward her.

She held up a hand to keep him at bay. "As long as I owe you? What are you saying? Is this what you brought me out here to talk about?"

"Let me explain the arrangement before you storm away," he said, ignoring her hand and stepping into her private space.

She shook her head vehemently. "No! I don't need an explanation. You paid for me once so you think you can do it again, permanently! You are out of your egotistical mind." Peering around him she glared at his counterparts. "All of you are out of your minds!"

"Jade," Linc said in a voice more stern than she'd ever heard it before. "We'll talk about this alone."

"No, we won't. You can stay right out here and continue to talk to your brothers. Three peas in a pod, three total idiots who are too wrapped up in what they have and who they are to let themselves ever trust anybody else. All three of you are sad and pathetic, thinking every woman is out to trap you. What a bunch of bull! If a woman is fool enough to want any one of you for a lifetime she's got to be just as crazy and demented as you are."

"Jade!"

"I don't want to hear your pitiful explanations," she yelled. "You can save them. And you two can rest assured that I am not trapping your beloved brother. My employment with him expires at midnight tonight, which is—" she looked down at her watch "—in about five minutes. Then I'll be completely out of your lives."

Tears burned at the back of her throat and she turned to leave before she made even more a fool out of herself. How could Linc have come up with such a territorial, egotistical, boneheaded idea like this? Was he really that shallow? That callous? She didn't know and she didn't care. She simply needed to get away from him as quickly as possible.

She left them standing there, her feet moving quickly over the ballroom floor as the clock was striking midnight. She really did feel like Cinderella now. In the distance she heard Beverly and Henry calling out to her but she didn't stop until she ran smack into Mario's huge frame.

"Ms. Jade, are you okay?"

She was shaking all over, the tears she didn't want to shed in front of Linc brimming at her eyes. "Yes," she said in a tiny voice that sounded nothing like her own. "Take me back to the house to get my things please, Mario."

Mario nodded then opened the door and helped her inside.

The ride back to the Donovan estate was the longest ride of her life. How had she been so stupid? Fantasizing that Lincoln Donovan could ever love her. He'd had no intention of there being any real commitment between them, but then he'd told her that already. He'd been completely honest about what he wanted from a woman. She was the one who'd changed. It was her fault. All of this was her fault. Another mistake in her long line of them.

For the billionth time in six months she cursed Charles. If he hadn't skipped out with her money she would have had no reason to be at the Gramercy and no reason to walk into Linc's life again. She would have never come to this gorgeous house and met these nice people...well, mostly nice people. She didn't know what to say about Adam and Trent. Maybe they were simply victims of the same stupidity as Linc but could she really blame them for trying to protect their brother?

She hiccupped a chuckle. Protect Linc from her? What a joke. She was the one who needed protection from him and his soft touches and smooth words. Slamming a fist against the seat she berated herself again for being twice a fool.

Chapter 12

"So you're the one leaving this time," Linc said from his perch against the doorjamb.

Jade paused for only a minute then resumed stuffing dresses into her suitcase. She'd changed out of her dress and now wore jeans and a wrinkled T-shirt. Her hair was tousled and from the set of her shoulders he could tell she was struggling to keep her composure. Hell, he was struggling to keep his. "Why are you leaving tonight instead of in the morning like we planned?"

She slammed the suitcase shut and snapped it

before pulling it off the bed. It appeared heavy and she struggled so he went to her side, attempted to grab it out of her hand. She pulled it back. For a minute they struggled, then he sighed. "You have got to be the most stubborn woman I've ever met."

She shot him an angry look. "I'll always be lumped together with that group of infamous females who are out to get you, won't I?"

He sighed with exasperation. "That's not what I meant."

"What did you mean, Linc? Why did you bring me here? Why didn't you simply call the police and have them haul my manipulating behind away when I couldn't repay your money?"

He hesitated, wanting to tell her that he couldn't let her walk out of his life again but refrained. "I didn't want you in jail."

"Oh, that's right, if I were in jail I couldn't repay you, either and it's all about the mighty Lincoln Donovan getting his money," she spat.

"I seem to recall you were getting something out of this deal, too." He stared at her incredulously. Could she have possibly been any more beautiful? He wanted to do and say anything that would keep her here, that would put them in that mood they were in before his brothers had interrupted. There was so much he wanted to say to her and yet he felt limited, restrained by thoughts of her dishonesty and his brothers' words of her using him. Placing Jade Vincent into a category—either of manipulator or possible wife material—was the hardest thing he'd ever been faced with. And for once in his life, Linc wasn't as focused as he needed to be.

"Jade, I don't want you to go like this. Let's talk about the other arrangement."

She frowned. "I don't want to hear about your damn arrangement."

"Let's be honest for a minute, Jade. We're good together. Why not keep this good thing by moving into an apartment? So what if I'm going to foot the bill? That was only until the money you took from my credit card was repaid. Everything would work out just fine as long as—"

"As long as every night I return to you, to your bed. Is that correct? So what does that make me, Linc? Your mistress? Your sex slave? What?"

Now she was starting to piss him off. He was offering her a rare opportunity and she acted like he'd just insulted her. "It makes you a damn smart businesswoman."

She shook her head and then he saw it. A lone tear, sliding down her face in slow motion, and something inside him broke. He reached out a hand to wipe that tear away and was devastated when she pulled back abruptly.

"No." She held up a hand to keep him away, shaking her head negatively as she did. "It would make me an even bigger fool than you. And that, Lincoln Donovan, I am not."

That one tear seemed to set the stage because now they flowed in full force. Linc couldn't explain the clutching at his heart and he couldn't explain why he so desperately needed her to stay. He was angry but he wasn't sure at whom. His fists clenched at his sides and his nostrils flared. "I'd rather be a fool than a thief," he said crisply.

She gasped as if he'd physically slapped her. Again he moved toward her, wanting to fold her into his arms, to protect her from…from whom? Himself? It didn't matter because she moved around him completely out of his reach as his feet now seemed planted to that very spot. Everything swirled around him, flashbacks of eight years ago in his dorm room with Jade mixed with memories of each day this week when he'd gotten to know her. Heat filled his body as helplessness and rage each battled for control.

"I'll give you that one," she said stiffly. "I used your credit cards to buy equipment for my spa. That was dishonest and I should have told you sooner. But let it be known that Jade Vincent does not steal. She doesn't have to. I spent a total of five thousand and eighty-eight dollars." With the back of her hand she swiped at the tears that stained her cheeks. "I'll pay you back every cent. Then I'll be out of your life forever."

Forever echoed in his head and Linc could swear the room tilted on its axis. He couldn't move.

Without another word Jade held her head high, her chin jutting forward and as beautiful as ever, walked out the door.

And out of Linc's life.

A week had passed and Linc was still at his parents' estate. His brothers had returned to their lives, but he had stayed. His mother had long since been filled in on what happened between he and Jade and for once in all his life she had barely spoken to him. Her anger and disappointment in him were apparent. Still, he wasn't prepared to admit he'd been wrong.

For seven nights he'd slept in that bed alone, smelling her scent, remembering her touch and each morning he awoke angrier and angrier with her. What did she want from him? He was offering her a once-in-a-lifetime chance. There were a million women who would kill for this opportunity to be with him.

But Jade Vincent apparently wasn't one of them.

And Jade Vincent was the one he wanted.

"How long is it going to take you?" Beverly asked when she entered his suite quietly.

Linc was sitting at his desk, papers strewn in front of him as if he were working but if asked he wouldn't have been able to explain what any of them were. "What? My work?"

"No." Beverly sat in the chair across from him. "For you to realize you were wrong and that you owe her an apology."

"I don't have time for this today, Mom." He wouldn't look up at her.

"Those papers on that desk don't have the answer, Lincoln."

With an exasperated sigh he finally leaned back in his chair and looked up. "And what answer would that be? Why she stole money from me?"

Beverly chuckled. "You know perfectly well that's not what she did."

"Then what did she, the all-perfect Jade, do, Mom? Since you'd like to pin this whole thing on me."

"She did what any red-blooded female would do when a man is foolish enough to hand her a credit card and tell her to go shopping. And she didn't even spend that much. I spend five thousand dollars in Saks alone." Beverly adjusted a bright yellow rose on the lapel of her white linen jacket.

"Five thousand dollars of your own money."

"Oh, please." She waved a hand at her son. "Whether the card has my name on it or Henry's it doesn't matter. And if you put your card in my hand it wouldn't matter, either. But that's not what you're so angry about. Is it, son?"

He looked away from her. How did mothers always know every damn thing? "It was all a mistake. I shouldn't have struck that deal with her in the first place."

"But you did. And I've spent the last few days trying to figure out why."

"Good. When you have it all figured out could you please keep it to yourself? I'm in no mood to hear it."

"Lincoln, did you forget that I'm the parent? I will do and say as I please and you will listen. Now whether or not you act on my words is completely up to you. But I'm pretty secure in the fact that I've raised an intelligent son and that ultimately you will do the right thing."

Linc sighed. There was no use arguing. Beverly Donovan was going to have her say.

"Eight years ago you made a mistake by walking away from that woman so when she walked into your casino, back into your life, you saw your second chance. But how to jump on that second chance without admitting that you were wrong in the first place? You know, I know how stubborn you are about admitting things. Her sister owed you money so she did the only thing she could to protect the one she loved. Coming here for the week was repayment. But it also got you what you really wanted, time with her again. Sure, you and your brothers are the Triple Threat Donovans." She chuckled.

"You didn't think I knew they called you that, did you?" Waving away his astonished look Beverly continued. "You foolishly thought one week would be enough. But then something else happened." Her voice softened. "You fell in love."

His mother only verbalized what he already knew to be true. He had fallen in love with Jade. But because he'd never pictured himself in love it was hard to swallow. "I knew going in that a week wouldn't be enough."

Beverly nodded. "Then you should have also known that Jade was not the type of woman for that arrangement you came up with. You should have known that her agreeing to come here for the week didn't have as much to do with her sister's debt as she believed it did. She wanted that time with you again, too. I tell you, young folk now days sure are book smart but don't have a lick of common sense."

"She wanted more right from the start," he said slowly. "I should have realized that. But she seemed so defensive, so determined to keep me at arm's length."

"I had a few opportunities to talk with her, Linc. She's been through a lot in her young life. She's had no choice but to perfect her defense skills. But she's come such a long way. She is determined to find her own happiness and she thought that would be with you."

"And I was too self-centered and selfish to see that. I told her that was my problem eight years ago."

"Obviously you haven't matured as much as you thought you had. Love is a funny thing, Lincoln. It sneaks up on you and bites you in the behind when you least expect it. But once it's got you, it doesn't let go."

Linc turned away, walked to the balcony and thrust his hands into his pockets. He was in love with Jade. There was no argument there. If truth be told the reason he'd been angry and kept himself secluded was that he didn't know how to go about telling her that now. He'd apologized for hurting her eight years ago and then he'd turned right around and done the same thing all over again. How could he ask for her forgiveness again?

"She's very angry with me."

Beverly rose, went to her son and placed a hand on his arm. "She loves you, too. I suspect she's loved you all these years. Women, even desperate women, don't give themselves completely to a man unless there are some feelings involved. Now, don't get me wrong, there are some manipulators out there, some users and some downright trifling females doing anything to get ahead. But Jade's not one of them and I think you know that."

Yes, he knew that. He knew very well what type of woman Jade was. Just as he knew what she wanted from a man. The very thing he was determined to give her.

The sign above the entrance read Happy Hands. The gold letters sparkled as did the glass door and front window. She knew because she'd shined them herself. Today she was unpacking the shipment of towels and inscribed robes that had arrived late yesterday afternoon when she was too pooped to do another thing.

Noelle had already begun working at the Gramercy even though she had less than desirable feelings about her boss. Jade had convinced her that it was a good opportunity. Noelle had a good mind but pushing her to go to college and to work at the spa probably wasn't the best path for her. Maybe that's why she'd been so resistant to it for so long. As part of her letting go Jade decided it

was time for Noelle to follow her own dream,
whatever that was.

She'd hired another part-time assistant, Jezell.
Jezell would be in shortly but for now Jade simply
enjoyed the peace and quiet. Jezell was twenty
years old and fresh out of massage school. She
talked a mile a minute and chewed gum on her
downtime, reminding Jade too much of Noelle.
That's probably why she'd hired her. Overall she
was a really nice woman with a lot of potential. Jade
just prayed she'd get used to the constant jabber-
ing.

After ten minutes of fighting with tape and box
cutters she finally had the package open and
pulled out one bright white terrycloth robe. She
held it in front of her and couldn't help a smile.
On the right hand side was the logo she'd finally
decided on, one hand over another in the center
of two peach-colored swirling *H*s. Pride welled up
in her chest and she felt the distinct prickle of
tears.

She was more than proud of her accomplish-
ments in life and had even come to grips with the
fact that things happened in the real world and
your character—which was so much more important than your social status—was formed through
those situations and how you dealt with them.

Three days after she'd left the Donovan home

Beverly Donovan had called her. They'd had lunch and for the first time in her life Jade felt as if she were on the same level as a rich and classy woman. She and Beverly had talked and even joked about the week she'd spent with Linc. At the end of the lunch Beverly had asked her what was the one thing she wished she could do over and Jade had instantly said she wouldn't have spent Linc's money as a form of revenge. In retrospect it had seemed like a good idea at the time but in the end she'd felt embarrassed and demeaned by the act. Beverly hadn't judged her by her answer but Jade could tell that wasn't what the woman wanted to hear. She promised to keep in touch and Beverly seemed pleased with that.

Overall Jade couldn't think of the week with Linc as a failure. It proved that she could survive, again. She'd given herself the entire Sunday after she'd left the Donovan estate to mourn the loss of Linc, again. But apparently that hadn't been enough. She missed him. Missed his presence, his commands, his challenges, his touches, his kisses. Oh man, did she miss his kisses.

He'd broken her heart again, but then she'd given it willingly, again. In the end it hadn't been their social status that came between them, it was his stubbornness and her pride. She couldn't be his live-in girlfriend. That was not the position she wanted in his life, or in any man's life for that matter. She deserved so much more. After being angry with Charles for months she'd finally resigned herself to the fact that he could have the money as long as he was out of her life. A lying cheater had no place in her heart. And neither did a self-centered, ambitious man who refused to see what he was passing up.

With a sigh she buried her face in the soft folds of the robe and screamed. She found that the little release on a daily basis helped her through. Now refreshed and renewed she pulled the robe away from her face preparing to seriously get started with the unpacking process and nearly screamed the walls down when she looked up to see him standing across the room.

"Hey, beautiful," Linc said with a slight grin.

Clutching the robe too tightly to her chest in the hopes that it would calm her pounding heart Jade frowned at him. Not because he'd scared her but because despite how angry she still wanted to be with him, he was still a dangerously good-looking man. Especially when he wore all black as he did today. Black slacks and a black T-shirt that hugged his upper body like a glove. He removed black sunglasses tucking them into his pocket.

"Hey, yourself." She frowned in his direction.

"We're not open yet. The sign out front clearly says ten o'clock." Which it did, but she'd left the door unlocked because she'd been bringing stuff in from her car.

Linc looked behind him to the sign posted in the window then back at her. "I know. I read it."

"Then why are you here?"

"I wanted to discuss another proposition with you."

Her knees wobbled as he crossed the room drawing closer by the second. She should move. She should say something. He was not supposed to be here. How was she supposed to forget about him if he wouldn't stay away?

She licked her lips then said in a shaky voice, "Linc, please. I can't do this with you anymore."

"Just give me a few minutes, Jade. A few minutes to state my case and if you still want me to leave after that I will. I'll do whatever you want."

She didn't want him to do whatever she wanted. She wanted him to follow his heart, to love her the way she loved him. And since that was not going to happen she didn't want anything. But if he'd come here he must have something to say. Whether or not she wanted to hear it remained to be seen. She looked past him through the window because staring at him caused an unbearable pain. She saw Mario standing in front of the car wearing the shades she'd given him and smiled. Mario waved and she waved back.

"I wish I could make you smile again," Linc said softly.

She instantly sobered. "Say what you have to say, Lincoln."

He nodded in agreement. "But before we go any further, I have something for you." With an extended hand he offered her an envelope.

She stared at it mutely. Her mind wrapped around the fact that it was an envelope but was too leery to be curious as to what it held.

"Go ahead, take it. It won't bite you." Linc dangled it toward her with a devilish grin.

"Like the serpent in the garden, whatever you offer turns out badly," she sighed.

"Ouch! I guess I deserved that." He took a step closer, lowered his voice. "I want you to take this, Jade. I promise it won't hurt you."

She looked into his eyes—big mistake—and found herself reaching for the envelope. She ripped it open and pulled out a check. Recognizing the name at the header she frowned. "Where did you get this?"

"From Charles Benson."

"But why? How?" Opening the envelope had been relatively easy compared to trying to figure out how she'd come to be holding a check from Charles in the exact amount he'd stolen from her account.

"I tracked him down. Told him he was a scumbag and that he owed you money." Linc shrugged. "He agreed."

Jade stared at him skeptically. "Charles would never agree. What did you do to him?" She couldn't believe it. He'd found out about Charles and instead of blaming her, instead of thinking it was her loss, he'd tracked him down and made Charles pay her back. And this was the man who called himself self-centered.

"Me? What did I do?" He feigned innocence, his act making her lips tilt momentarily in a smile. "Okay, okay. I may have threatened him a bit. But he really did come around quickly. Especially after he found out Trent was an ex-Seal."

A giggle did escape then and Jade fanned the check in front of her face for a moment. "Thank you," she said slowly.

"Don't mention it. I didn't come here for gratitude, Jade."

"Then what do you want?" she asked nervously. He was looking at her with hunger in his eyes. But there was something else about him that she couldn't quite explain or wasn't willing to accept.

"Like I said, I have another proposition for you."

She shook her head quickly. "I'm not interested in any more of your propositions."

He moved closer until they stood only a breath away. "I think you'll be interested in this one."

She huffed, a renewed sense of discord coming to life between them. "Oh, you are still so very sure of yourself, aren't you? Well, I'll have you know that I am not impressed by you or your high-handedness, Lincoln Donovan!" She emphasized each word by poking a finger into his chest. He hadn't budged. "I'm sick and tired of you thinking that the world revolves around you and what you want. And while I'm on the subject just let me say that if you continue to think you can sleep with women and then turn them away on that foolish excuse that you are never marrying, then one day, one woman is going to be time enough for you to make you pay for all the heartache you've caused."

He grabbed her wrists and her mouth snapped shut. "You've paid me back already."

Out of breath and instantly heated by both his proximity and his touch Jade blinked before asking, "What? How?"

"I've been absolutely miserable since the night

you walked out on me. Now I know how you must have felt that night I left." He eased his grip on her wrists then lifted them to his mouth and kissed the backs of her hands.

"Don't," she whispered.

"Don't what? Don't tell you how sorry I am that I hurt you again? Or don't tell you that it's taken all this time for me to figure out I was an idiot for letting you go not once, but twice?"

She was stunned into complete silence.

"Because that's the absolute truth, Jade. I never wanted this feeling because I knew I couldn't control it. I knew once it happened I'd be lost. My identity and all I worked for would be lost because this feeling would take precedence over everything."

"I...I don't understand."

His thumbs stroked over her hands as he pulled her closer until her breasts brushed against his chest. "I thought I had my life all planned out. That all I needed was success. But then when I had that success I still felt incomplete. And then you walked back into my life and instantly filled that gap. It was stupid of me to think that I could have you without giving myself totally. You said you wanted a man to love you so much he couldn't think straight and that's exactly what you deserve."

"What are you saying?"

"I'm saying that I was wrong to offer you an apartment and a relationship with no real commitment. No real feelings."

She wanted to pull away to stop this twister of emotion from whirling through her. She was angry with him. She was brokenhearted. She was not happy that he was here and she did not believe a word he was saying. Yet she heard herself asking, "Why?"

"You were looking for a knight in shining armor to come and rescue you. Instead, you're the one who rescued me."

Tears welled in her eyes and she began shaking her head in disbelief. Cupping her face in his hands he stilled her motions. "Yes, you did. If you hadn't come into the casino that day I never would have seen you again and I never would have accepted what I knew eight years ago. That I'd fallen in love with you."

"There would have been someone…else," she stuttered through her tears.

His thumbs caught the falling drops, wiping them away. "No. There would have been no one else. Because I've loved you from the start. It just took me a minute to realize it."

"You were too stubborn." She giggled then slapped a hand over her mouth.

He chuckled. "I guess you're right."

He moved her hand and traced her bottom lip. Her heart stilled with anticipation. She didn't know what brought him here and she didn't care. She didn't know who had made him see that he was wrong because she knew that Linc was too in control to ever see his own errors or faults, but she didn't care. He was here now and that's all that mattered…well, that wasn't all that mattered.

"So, I'll ask you again, Linc, what are you doing here?"

"I've come to make you an offer you can't refuse. But first," he said, putting a small amount of distance between them, "I need to tell you that I am so in love with you that not only can't I think straight, I can't work or eat. And my mother threatened to disown me if I didn't come to my senses and make things right with you. So I hope that with every beautiful ounce of your being that you can forgive me for messing up," he added a smile, "again."

She smiled. She couldn't help it. She'd waited so long to hear these words from him. She'd dreamed of the possibility, prayed for the reality and now here he was. And she was absolutely clueless as to what she should say. "I don't know what to say, this is all so…so…"

"Do you love me, Jade?" He kissed her palms. "Please tell me it's not too late."

"You're wrong, Linc."

His head shot up with lightning-fast speed. "Excuse me?"

"You are my knight in shining armor," she said, wrapping her arms around his neck pulling him closer in the process. "You have saved me from another broken heart. And if I didn't already love you, I would have fallen the moment you walked through that door. "

Linc smiled, dipping his head to kiss her. Long and slow the kiss lingered on, their old rhythm renewed with the confession of love.

Then Linc abruptly pulled away. "But that's not what I'm here for," he said, a huge grin spreading across his face.

"It's not?" She blinked. "Then what are you here for? Oh, your new proposition. What is it?"

With a hand at the nape of her neck he dropped a kiss on her forehead then one on her ear and whispered, "Double or nothing."

She frowned. "You want me to spend two weeks with you now?"

He laughed. "No, baby. I want you to spend forever with me."

Epilogue

The ballroom of the Gramercy casino was decorated in shades of peach and white as the newlyweds made their way from the stretch limousine that Linc insisted on renting, driven by Mario, of course.

They'd exchanged vows in a private ceremony on the Donovan estate, at Beverly's request, then headed straight for Vegas for a gala reception, at Linc's request. He wanted the world to see that he'd taken a wife, effectively putting an end to the Triple Threat Brothers.

Adam and Trent, although they'd accepted Jade with sincere apologies for overreacting and butting into her and Linc's relationship, were ecstatic about their brother's happiness but in no way ready to concede themselves.

"To each his own," Adam said holding up a glass of champagne.

Linc smiled. "Your time will come, little brother." He lifted his glass, too.

Trent laughed. "I known mine won't. You two are crazy for even entertaining the idea." His was the final glass lifted to clatter with the other two in a toast to their future.

"Who said I was entertaining the idea?" Adam asked while his brothers drank.

Both Linc and Trent laughed at the fraught sound of his voice. "Calm down, bro. It's not as bad as we thought," Linc offered.

"How would you know? You've been married all of three hours."

Glancing across the room Linc caught his wife's eye and smiled. "And it's been a fabulous three hours. Now if you gentlemen will excuse me…" He handed Trent his glass and made his exit.

"Look at him." Adam nodded in the direction Linc had gone. "Totally whipped."

Trent downed his glass of champagne and Linc's. "Yeah, I know. That's why I'm not even considering the thought."

"Me, neither," Adam said more to himself since Trent had abandoned him to make another trip to the bar.

He didn't want another drink but he did need some air. All this marriage talk was starting to bother him. For as long as he could remember Linc had taught him the ins and outs of dating women. His firm rule had been never to trust them. He'd made the mistake of not listening to Linc once and had been severely bruised. He vowed not to make that mistake again.

In the hallway he inhaled deeply and exhaled. He was happy for Linc and Jade. They made a good couple and he knew that Jade would make his brother happy. But he didn't need that type of happiness. He took one step forward and attempted to turn the corner when he collided with her.

Linc and Jade were trying to sneak off to find a moment to themselves when she spotted Adam, his hands on a woman's shoulders in the hallway.

"Well, well, well, would you look at that?"

Linc followed her gaze. "Look at what?"

"Adam's found a friend."

Linc recognized the gleam in her eyes and frowned. "Don't even think about it. Adam is never getting married. That you can count on."

Jade lifted her left hand, dangling her fingers so that the four-karat marquise-cut wedding ring sparkled in his face. "That's what they all say."

* * * * *

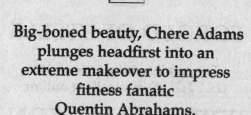

Big-boned beauty, Chere Adams
plunges headfirst into an
extreme makeover to impress
fitness fanatic
Quentin Abrahams.

But perhaps it's Chere's curves that
have caught Quentin's eye?

All About Me

Marcia King-Gamble

AVAILABLE JANUARY 2007
FROM KIMANI™ ROMANCE

Love's Ultimate Destination

Available at your favorite retail outlet.